The
Unfinished
Angel

SHARON CREECH

The Unfinished Angel

JOANNA COTLER BOOKS
An Imprint of HarperCollinsPublishers

The Unfinished Angel
Copyright © 2009 by Sharon Creech

www.harpercollinschildrens.com

Library of Congress Cataloging-in-Publication Data
Creech, Sharon.
    The unfinished angel / Sharon Creech. — 1st ed.
       p.   cm.
    Summary: In a tiny village in the Swiss Alps, an angel meets an American girl named Zola who has come with her father to open a school, and together Zola and the angel rescue a group of homeless orphans, who gradually change everything.
    ISBN 978-0-06-143097-8
    [1. Angels—Fiction. 2. Orphans—Fiction. 3. Villages—Fiction.
4. Switzerland—Fiction.] I. Title.
PZ7.C8615Un 2009   2009002796
[Fic]—dc22   CIP
                                         AC

Typography by Michelle Gengaro-Kokmen
❖
13 14 15 16 17 OPM 12 11 10 9 8 7 6 5 4 3

Revised paperback edition, 2013

Once upon a time there was an angel,
and the angel was me.
PEARL B. BENJAMIN

In memory of four sparkly ones:
Dennis W. Creech
Mary Crist Fleming
Kate McClelland
Kathy Krasniewicz

Contents

PEOPLES

Peoples are strange!
     The things they are doing and saying—sometimes they make no sense. Did their brains fall out of their heads? And why so much saying, so much talking all the time day and night, all those words spilling out of those mouths? Why so much? Why don't they be quiet?

WHAT I'VE BEEN DOING

Me, I am an angel. I am supposed to be having all the words in all the languages, but I am not. Many are missing. I am also not having a special assignment. I think I did not get all the training.

What is my mission? I think I should have been told. I have been lolling around in the stone tower of Casa Rosa, waiting to find out. I am free to come and go in the mountain villages, free to float along the promenade on the lake, free to swish up through the Alps to mountain huts, free to spend days and nights floating and swishing. This floating and swishing I like.

It's true I have my hands full from time to time with Signora Divino and her grandson, Vinny, neither of them the slightest bit "divino" these days: cranky and bad-tempered, raining soot on everyone else's head. Signora Divino, she snip-snip gossips and causes trouble between the other peoples, and her grandson, Vinny, with the shaggy hair is causing the mischief and blaming the other boys, and he listens to no one, no one, you hear me? No one. I pinch him sometimes.

But is that my purpose? Solely to look after the Divinos and keep them from heaping misery on the other people types and giving them a pinch from time to time? I don't think so.

Do the other angels know what they are doing? Am I the only confused one? Maybe I am unfinished, an unfinished angel.

The Invaders

Sometimes I want to throw pinecones at Divino heads, and more heads, too: those peoples—the American man and his daughter—who moved into Casa Rosa. Where they come from, out of the green? Who lets them come here into my casa?

The American, Mr. Pomodoro, is tall and linky with a rubbery face that moves his cheeks and nose and eyes when he talks and even when he doesn't talk. He says he is starting a school here, and not just any school, but "the best of the best." He tells Signora Divino, his neighbor, "We will bring all the children from all over the world and we will live in harmony!"

Is he kidding?

"We will have Turks and Germans," Mr. Pomodoro

says, "Iraqis and French, Russians and Chinese, Swiss and Dutch, Koreans and Brazilians, Israelis and Swedes, *et cetera!*" He squinches his eyes and nose in happy thoughts of all these peoples.

Signora Divino looks as if she has swallowed a goose. She does not seem to like the thought of all those peoples in this little village on the mountain. "Will you also have Americans?" she asks.

"Americans?" Mr. Pomodoro glances up at my stone tower and moves his lips around as if he is tasting them from the inside and says, "Of course."

Signora Divino lifts one bent finger and aims it at him. "There are snakes at Casa Rosa," she says.

Mr. Pomodoro blinks. "Snakes?"

"Many snakes."

"Many?"

The Signora's finger crawls through the air. "Many, many black snakes." She smiles.

Mr. Pomodoro smiles, too. "Thank you," he says. "Thank you for that information."

THE DAUGHTER

Mr. Pomodoro has a daughter. At least, I assume she is his daughter, arriving at the same time, staying in the same house, but she does not resemble him. Maybe this is a good thing. And where is the mother? I see no mother. And there is a picture of a young boy on the mantel. Where is he?

I do not know about this daughter, what sense to make of her. She is called Zola and is skinny like a twig-tree, with hair chip-chopped in a startling way. Her eyes—gray with large black poppils in the middle—her eyes are big and round like a cow's. She appears, over-all—I don't know how to say—like maybe a fawn who grew up with humans. Or a chickadee who was raised by crows. I don't know. You are not understanding what I am saying, are you?

While Signora Divino asks Mr. Pomodoro many questions, Zola scouts for snakes. Signora Divino wants to know why the Mr. Pomodoro creature came here, to this village. "Why?" she asks. "Why? Why?"

"For a new start!" he says, with the happy rubber cheeks. Then his shoulders sag. "I am weary."

"Of what you are weary?" presses nosy Signora Divino.

"Where should I start? I am weary of malls and merchandise and sales and rude drivers and cell phones and blasting music and big cars and fast food and you know those marshmallow candies that look like animals?"

"No, I don't know what you are saying."

"Well, I don't like those."

"Oh," says Signora Divino. "Anything else?"

Zola, who is in the bushes hunting for snakes, seems to reply for Mr. Pomodoro with an air puff that escapes from her feet up through her whole body to her mouth. *"Foof."*

Signora Divino turns toward the *foof* and then returns her stare to Mr. Pomodoro, who says, "I am weary of *incivility.*"

It is a precious-sounding word, and I hear another

foof from Zola in the bushes.

"*You* know," Mr. Pomodoro continues, "bad manners, burping, crude language, that sort of thing."

"Uck!" Signora Divino says. "Idiots! Cretins!"

My Tower

Maybe my tower—the tower of Casa Rosa—is not the most attractiful or the most specialty tower in Switzerland. It is just a tower, after all, like so many other towers in the Ticino, this southern part of Switzerland. The casa is pink, like so many other casas, but the stone tower that rises three more stories above it is the color of its stone—how you call it? Tan? The color of straw in the winter? Of coffee with very much milk?

It is a tower that stands tall and upending like a good soldier, for nearly four hundred years, not wobbling or falling down. At the top of the tower is an open balcony with a low wall all around and a tile roofling overhead. There are no windows. You reach out and there is the air, just there. You are high, high above the other houses and the only things as high are a few trees and, down the road, the tall stickly spire of the church. The only thing in this balcony is a gauzy hammock, a light and airful place for me to loll about.

Beneath the balcony is a tiny square room, exactly the size of the balcony above it. In this room are two trip doors: One leads up to the balcony and one leads down to the room below. Also in this room is a narrow cot covered with a worn feather duvet, and a small desk with a candle on it.

The room beneath that one with the cot is again a tiny square, exactly the size of the room and balcony above it. In this room is nothing but dead spiders and flies; the trip door in the ceiling which goes up into the room above; and a short door (for like a shrunken man) which leads out onto a narrow, narrow landing and to curving narrow steps down into the main house below.

So, maybe you might think it is nothing specialful, this tower, but to me it is the finest of all the towers in all the world. From the balcony I can see mountains in a ring all around, a circle of mountains, and on the very top of those mountains most of the year is white, white snow, and below the mountains is a blue-green lake, and above the mountains at night is a blue-black sky all pokeled with blue-white stars. From my tower, I can see all the casas in the village and I can see all the peoples coming and going. I can see all the birds flying in the air and the creatures crawling on the ground.

Only once in four hundred years did someone live in the room beneath the balcony, the one with the narrow cot. A servant girl lived there. She had summoned me, and I stayed in the tower watching over her until another angel came and took her away. I did not see that angel because I was outside collecting figs, but I heard the flooshing and saw the golden light. After that, no one ever stayed in that room except for me. Sometimes when the wind is blowering hard and bellowing like a bull, I slip through the trip door and into the bed with the feather duvet. An angel does not *need* a bed, but sometimes I think the bed needs an angel.

I do not know what I mean. The words are maybe not right.

ZOLA

~~~∞~~~

On her first night in Casa Rosa, Zola climbs the narrow, ziggy stone steps to the tower and clambers through the tripping door up to the balcony. I am lolling at the time, draped over the windowsill, smashing figs. Below me are the blue hills slipping down to the lake, and above floats a chalky white balloon moon, which is sending light beams down to the deep blue lake.

Zola does not seem afraid. I'm not in the definite that she can see me at all, but right away she says, "*Ciao*," and leans over the sill, studying the smashed figs dripping down the stone. "An angel?" she adds.

There you have it. She knows right away. Most peoples don't. Sometimes young children seem to see or feel *something*, but they do not have the words for what they see. Usually those children blink or squint as if the light is too bright.

One child once pointed right at me and said, "Pipple! Pipple!"

His mother paid no attention, as if maybe the child said silly words all day long.

The boy squinched his eyes nearly closed. "Pipple!"

"What *are* you saying?" his mother asked. "Pickle? You want a pickle? You'll have to wait until we get home." As she tugged the boy along, he swingled his head around to see me. "Pipple? Pipple?"

"When we get home!" his mother said, not very kindly.

But now, in the tower, here is the Zola girl, and she seems not at all surprised to see me, and she is saying, "An angel?"

"I live here," I say.

"Hmm. And you plan on staying here?"

Honestly! Peoples, what do they think? They can barge in and move angels out?

"Yes. I *live* here."

"Mmm. Well, then, if you are going to continue to live here, I assume you will help me."

I do not like her assuming that I will help her. I don't have to do any such thing.

"I bet you are a clever angel," she says. "*Extremely*

clever. You're a bit young, but no younger than me. . . ."

Peoples think they know everything! I am maybe hundreds of years old!

Zola smashes a fig against the wall, much as I do. "An angel in our tower is certainly better than snakes in our tower."

Our tower? Peoples!

Zola smills, smuggles, what is that word? What is it, that word for the happy teeth?? Smule? Smale? Smile? Smile! She does the smile, showing her white teeth, mostly straight and enough large. In the moonlight, her crippy-croppy hair shines silver and blue.

Zola says, "I guess we'll be a team. I am *truly* and *deeply* honored."

Honored? Truly? Deeply? Well, that is a pinch better.

As Zola turns to zag her way back down the steps, she adds, "Feel free to hover about"—she waves a fig-smudged hand through the air—"and get the feel of things. There will be a lot of activity around here. Intervene whenever you like!" With that, she disappears down the steps.

Peoples! *Hover?* I do not hover! *Feel free?* Of course I will feel free, whether she tells me to or not. *Intervene?* Of course I will intervene . . . if I *choose* to.

WHAT IS AN ANGEL?

An angel is supposed to be a happy being, no? Angels are supposed to float about bringing love and goodwill and protection and good fortune, no? I do not know where I got these ideas. Maybe they are wrong. Me, I am not feeling all that cheerful with all the peoples around, and I am not finding many peoples deserving of the splashes of love and good fortune, even if I knew how to splash and where to get the love and good fortune.

I am only feeling floaty when I am swishing up into the mountains to see the goats. Goats do not talk. They mostly are chewing the grassy plants and occasionally saying *Beh, beh, beh,* in a low, cricky voice.

It must be that I did not get the right training for the angels that work with peoples. Maybe I was supposed to be a different kind of angel, one of those that swoop down from above when peoples die and then lead them up to heaven. I think that kind of angel only does transport. Maybe I was supposed to be a transport angel but by mistake was dropped off as a ground angel.

Maybe you think I should just fly up to heaven and ask some questions, but it is not that easy. I do not know where heaven is nor where the angel training center is nor where any other angels are. And yes, I have looked.

Maybe I could wait by the bed of a dying person and then when a transport angel comes, I could follow the angel and the dead person up to heaven. I wonder if the transport angels ever make mistakes and take the wrong peoples, ones who are not actually dying.

THE FASHION OF ZOLA

~~~~~~~~

I tell you, Zola is not resembling other young peoples up here in the mountains. She wears many clothes on top of other ones, like this: three dresses, one atop each other, or sometimes two skirts under a third and layers of scarves around her middle and her neckle and in her hair. It is not even cold out, I am telling you. It is summer.

Everything is very bright colors, some colors I do not know the names for, more than raspberry and emerald and turquoise and periwinkle (that is a color, right?), yellows like the sun and the birds, and oranges like the apricots and the tangerines and the melons. And rainbows of ribbons on her wrists and ankles and neckle and in her hair. I thought maybe she did not have the cupboard for to put her clothes in and so she had to wear everything she owns, but there is much space in this house. Maybe she cannot choose and just keeps adding clothing until it surpleases her.

What to make of this peacock girl marching along swinging her arms and singing into the air?

Today, on the path up to Montagnola, Zola passes Signora Mondopoco making her slow, hunched way down the hill.

Zola stops to greet the Signora. *"Ciao!"*

Signora Mondopoco peeks at Zola with all her clothes and colors and then she glances down at her own feets. It is not cold outside, but Signora Mondopoco is wearing short boots with a fringe of brown fur sticking out the tops. The Signora points to the fur and says, "Baa, baa, baa. Is real!"

"Fur, fleece? From a lamb?" Zola presses her dainty hands to her chest. "How especially perfect," she says, quite seriously, as if Signora Mondopoco has just offered a crucial fact of existence.

Later, Zola clabbers up to the tower, sticking flowers in her hair and dancing about and singing, "Turenia, Bedenia, my name is Eugenia."

"Not Zola?" I say.

"Today I am Eugenia." She is moving in a slowly liquidy way as if her arms and legs were on long strings pulled by an invisible being. "Turenia, Bedenia, my name is Eugenia. Have you seen my Row-row-rowena?"

"No, I have not."

"Sa-la, then," she says, swillowing back to the ladder hole.

"Sa-la," I say.

THOSE DIVINOS

From the tower this morning just before the light
crawls up behind the mountain, I spy Signora
Divino in her housecoat and her muddy garden boots
dragging a big black snake into the yard of Casa Rosa—
my yard and the American Pomodoro yard now, too. She
shoves the snake into our woodpile and says, "*Ciao, ciao.
Avanti!*"

The snake is not fast moving in the chilly morning,
but it manages to keep pace with Signora Divino, following her back to her yard. She turns and sees it. "Acka!"
She says some other words, too, words no one should
hear, they are so ugly. She picks up the snake and drags
it back into the yard of Casa Rosa and says, "*Avanti,*

avanti!" She spits at the snake to show she means business corporate.

I drop a pinecone from the tower and it lands on the Signora's head. It does not hurt her, but it makes her mad. She shakes her fist at the air and says some more ugly words.

Later in the morning a banana peel flies over the hedge from the Divino yard into our yard. You do not do this in Switzerland. You do not make garbage fly around.

Next comes a rotten apple. *Splut!* A soft fig. *Splut!* Two pieces of salami. *Suh. Suh.*

I am just getting ready to toss a pinecone when Zola zigs out of the house and yells into the bushes. "Stop that, whoever is doing that! Stop it right now!"

Another fig. *Splut.*

Zola, she surprises me, she turns into a bull cow and blasts through the bushes, and I have to float fast so I can see her lean toward Vinny and say, "Listen, you piffling toad, you keep your garbage in your own yard, you hear me?"

The piffling toad steps away from her and says, "*Non capisco!* Ha!" He doesn't know what she has said.

This makes Zola very mad. She says, "You *capro!* You *porco!* You *gallo!*"

I guess she does not know the word for *toad.* Instead,

she has called Vinny a goat, a pig, and a rooster.

Vinny says, "*Pomodoro* means *tomato*!" Then he runs into his grandmother's house and slams the door.

Zola Pomodoro stares at the door. "Nuthead!"

HAIRS AND FEETS

You won't believe this, but there are peoples who pay money to other peoples to wash their hairs and even to paint colors on their toes. Is really! And in the same world of peoples there are other peoples who have to crawl in the dirt scrounging for a measly piece of garbage to eat. I am not fabbagrating! Don't get me started.

At night I swish in the heads of the peoples with the clean hairs and feets, showing them the peoples crawling in the dirt, but in the morning when the clean peoples wake up they have already forgotten. I think maybe it is my fault that they forget so quick and so it is my fault that there are peoples who have to crawl in the dirt. I am not knowing enough. What are the other angels doing?

The Matter *Urgente*

I am leaning over the balcony of my tower watching Signora Divino gather fat orange slugs in her yard. She is wearing her sturdy black shoes and her plain black dress and over the top of the dress is a pink bedjacket. This is shockful because Signora Divino only and always wears black to show that she was once a married lady but now her husband is dead. But here she is with the pink bedjacket. Signora Divino does not wear pink and peoples do not normally wear bedjackets outside.

It is while I am wondering about this pink bedjacket that Zola clabbers up the winding steps to the tower and says—without any politeness of hello or *ciao*—"Angel! You have to do something about the kids in the barn!"

I do not like it when peoples tell me I *have* to do

something. It makes me want to *not do* the something. I
pretend I am not hearing today.

"Angel! Why haven't you done something about the
kids in the barn?"

I pretend I am studying the cobwebs under the roof.
Zola, she is all orange and yellow and turquoise, with
three skirts and a blouse and a shawl and a purple ribbon wound around her ankle and green feathers in her
hair. I glance at Signora Divino, gathering slugs in her
pink bedjacket. The pink bedjacket does not appear so
strange now.

"Angel!"

Zola is not going to let me alone, I can see. I am not
stupido.

"What barn?" I say. "What kids?"

"On the path up to Montagnola," she says. "That
ancient barn."

"What ancient barn?" All the buildings here are
ancient, but there are no barns left in the village.

"On the path going up the hill. Across from the pink
house. On the right. Up—you know—up there." She
wivvles her arm toward the path and the hill.

"Oh," I say. "That shid—shad—shed broken thing?
That used to hold chickens? That thing?"

Zola gruntles, not very happy. "I don't know what
you call it or what used to be there, but I'm talking about

the kids that are there now."

"What kids?"

"Angel! You're supposed to know everything!"

I am? This is a little shock to me. No, it is a big shock. Because I am not knowing many, many things.

Zola does not look too happy with me. She says, "There are kids there, living there, in that dark and dirty and cold place. A bunch of them. Eight or ten. Maybe more. They're skinny and hungry and dirty. It is extremely tragical."

"Why are they living there?"

"Angel!" Zola holds her head in her hands as if I am giving her a very big headache. "That's what I'm asking *you*. You're supposed to know these things. You're supposed to fix these things."

Know *and* fix? How does Zola know these things? Why does she know them and I don't? I am not feeling so good.

A PUZZLEMENT

I float *rapido* up to the shid-shad-shed which used to hold the chickens of the family Polterini and before that many long years ago the chickens and very nasty rooster of the family Zucchini, and before that—well, I am only saying that I have been around a long time and I know exactly this place Zola is talking about, and I would know if there were childrens living there, especially if the childrens were skinny and hungry and dirty. I do not like peoples to be hungry. Especially I do not like them to be hungry when other peoples give money to someones for painting their toes.

But this is Switzerland, and childrens should not go hungry here. I think it is against the law. So it is impossible what Zola says, right?

And see? The shad is empty. No childrens. When Zola arrives, I say, "Empty."

"Are you sure?" Zola scrambles over the fence and up the hill and peers in through the straggly wire fencing. "They're probably out scavenging for food," she says.

I make a snort sound, which Zola does not like.

"Angel, you are disappointing me!"

What? This hurts my feeling.

Zola is standing with her hands on her hips and giving me a muddy look. "Angel! Come back when it is dark. You'll see." Zola runs down the path. I think she's supposed to be helping Mr. Pomodoro get the school ready for students from all over the world who are going to be nice to each other and make the world peaceful.

I wonder how they think this is going to happen, the peaceful part. I have been watching peoples a long time and they get mad at one another very easily. They are not calming down.

At night I return to the chicken place, not expecting to find anything except maybe some snakes and bats, but to my surprisement there are kids there, about eight or nine of them, skinny and dirty. They are huddled in a corner under one torn blanket and they are gnawing at a loaf of bread. The youngest one, maybe he is five or six years old, is sniveling. "Mama," he whimpers. "I want Mama."

"*Zitti!*" says a bigger kid. "Somebody'll hear you and then we'll all get carted off to jail."

This makes the youngest cry harder. I float over and beam warm beams down on them. Poor little things. No mamas. Cold. In the dark.

I am being confused. Where do they come from? How long have they been there? Why haven't *I* seen them? I am not knowing what to do.

VINNY EXPLOSION

That night I do not sleep. I float here and there and far up in the mountains where the goats are closing their eyes and leaning against each other. I float past the huts and meadows and bridges and streams. I peer in the chicken shads and the pigpens. There are chickens and pigs there. No childrens. The childrens are in the huts and casas with their mamas and papas where they belong.

The next morning I whiz south, back to my tower in the Ticino. The tower is sitting in a cloud. It is the misty driplets that come some mornings and wrap around the village so that all you can see around you is the white cloud. You cannot see the mountains opposite, you cannot see the houses on the hillside or even the roads or the lake down below. The sounds are miffled, as if a big scarf is wrapped around the village.

When I float through the house, I see Mr. Pomodoro in a baggy robe standing in front of the mantel, staring at the photo of the little boy. Mr. Pomodoro's hair is in bed mess and his shoulders are aslump. He puts his finger on the photograph in such a tender way that you can see his heart is very big for this little boy. I float back to my tower to wonder about the boy.

It is so quiet, quiet, until Vinny bangs on a metal bucket and his grandmother, Signora Divino, shouts at him to shut down—*"Zitti! Zitti!"*—but he keeps on banging. Then Zola joggets out of her house and bellows into the hedge, "Stop that racket, you artichoke!" But the artichoke doesn't stop, and Zola pushes through the gate and grabs the metal bucket and throws it into the pond of frogs.

Signora Divino hobbles out of her house in her pink bedjacket (again!) and says many ugly words to Zola in Italian and Zola says them right back at her, even though I do not think Zola knows what they mean.

Signora Divino is *molto* insulted that Zola has spoken to her in this rude way. "I tell your father!" Signora Divino threatens.

"I have no father," Zola says. "I am an orphan and my name is Fillipa Millipa."

I am thinking angels should not be having head-aches, but I am having one, very pounding one.

Zola shouts up at the tower, "Can't you do anything about these morons?"

I wish Zola would not be talking to me like that, out in the air. Signora Divino and her grandson, Vinny, glance up at the tower and then at each other and then at Zola. They do not see me.

Zola says to Vinny, "If you want to bang on some-thing, why don't you bang on some drums?"

Vinny stamps his foot like a horse and makes his neck very straight like a goose. "I *do* drums," he says. "*Molto* years. *Molto* good."

Zola presses her small hand to her heart theatrically. "I most sincerely doubt that," Zola says, and she leaves, which makes Vinny even madder, because he is left with only his grandma to give the show-off to.

Zola zips right up to the tower. "Angel! Where were you last night? And what are you doing about the chil-dren in the chicken barn?"

This Zola is a lot bossy.

IL BEASTO

I forgot to say about *il beasto*. First, I tell you that I am
in peace with the birdies and the froggies and the
toads and the kittens and the puppies and the lizards, all
of those creatures, just like I am in peace with the mountains and the trees and the flowers, but let's not get too
mushy. I tell you that so you know that I am not like the
peoples who hate everything and complain all day short
or long. Those peoples are sad.

Il beasto is the dog of Signora Divino: a bitsy poky
dog you might accidentally step on, a barking, nippy-
snappy noise *macchina*. The noise is bigger than the dog.
The noise makes you want to kill it.

Like this it goes, just when you are enjoying the air
and the mountains of view: *arf, arf, arf, arf, arf, arf, arf,*

arf, arf, arf, arf, arf, arf, arf, arf, arf, arf, arf, arf, arf, arf, arf, arf, arf, arf, arf, arf, arf. Then it stops and you are so happy for the quiet that you could cry. But you are only happy for a minute because there it goes again: *arf, arf, arf, arf, arf, arf, arf, arf, arf, arf, arf, arf, arf, arf, arf, arf, arf, arf, arf, arf, arf, arf, arf, arf, arf, arf, arf, arf.*

Peoples in the village try to tell Signora Divino that the dog's *arf*ing makes them crazy in the head, but Signora Divino is without enough ears. She says, "What? I can't hear you. What?" And so people stand there barking like the dog and she says, "Whatsa matter with you?"

Zola and Mr. Pomodoro are not happy with the *arf, arf, arf* of Signora Divino's *beasto*. They want to kill it.

Zola stands on the balcony of her bedroom and shouts down at the *arf*ing *beasto*: "Be quiet! Shut up! Stop it! I'm going to kill you!"

Mr. Pomodoro stands on the balcony of his bedroom and shouts down at the *arf*ing *beasto*: "Be quiet! Shut up! Stop it! I'm going to kill you!"

And Signora Divino, without enough ears, gathers slugs in her garden and brings them and the snakes into the yard of our casa when she thinks we do not see.

MR. POMODORO

I am not sure what to make of Mr. Pomodoro. Because he is so tall and linky and rubbery, he seems sometimes like a boy, knocking into tables and doorways, his big muddy boots clomping on the tile floors. He will smile one minute and frown the next, squinch his nose, tilt his head left and then right, scrunch his mouth.

Other times, he appears more like a man: He spreads books and papers and archno-techno drawings on the table and makes notes with his sharpened pencil. "Mm" and "ah" and "erm," he mumbles. He tapples rapidly into his dimputer, *tapple, tapple, tapple,* pauses, looks up, ponders the ceiling, resumes tappling.

When Zola wanders in and out, he is offlivious to her. She seems accustomed to this. He is not ignoring her, exactly. It is more as if he can only do one thing at a time. I think maybe she enjoys the freedom. I don't know why I have that impression; maybe it is because she does not seem sad or miserable or in any way unhappy.

Today, for instance, Mr. Pomodoro finishes his reading and tappling, turns off his dimputer, stands up, and goes to the bottom of the staircase. He listens and then he climbs the stairs and clomps down the hallway, stopping at each room and briefly gazing in.

At Zola's doorway, he sees her sprawled on the floor with her feet up on the bed, a stack of paperback novels beside her and one in her hand, which she is reading. On the cover is an island with a single palm tree and footprints in the sand.

Mr. Pomodoro stretches his rubbery mouth, cracks his knuckles, says, "Well, then," and moves on down the hall. I don't think they are mad at each other, Zola and Mr. Pomodoro. It is more as if he does not know quite what to do with this colorful child and is relieved that she is content to be on her own.

Downstairs again, Mr. Pomodoro unpacks a few things from one of the many boxes stacked by his desk. He unwraps a small photo, smiles at it, takes it to the mantel, and places it beside the one of the boy. It is a photo of a young woman, maybe twenty. Mr. Pomodoro presses a finger to her picture and then turns to the little boy's picture and does the same.

I am about to float on up to my balcony when I notice Mr. Pomodoro return to his desk and open one of its deep drawers. I slap my headfore! What I see inside reminds me of a tale Zola told me. When was this? I don't remember. Before the shad problem.

We were up in the tower, me and Zola, smashing figs. We watched her father as he packled in the garden below. Zola says, "Angel, Angel, I will tell you about a boy. Would you like that?"

Truly, I have no grand interest, but it is a lazy day and so I say, "Tell away."

Zola licks fig juice from her fingers. "There once was a young boy with nine brothers and sisters. His family lived in a crowded, crumbling house at the bottom of a hill. There was never much food to eat in that house with all its children, but one day his father brought home a box of chocolate-covered cookies. Have you ever eaten a chocolate-covered cookie, Angel?"

"Me? No, no, I don't eat cookies."

"Oh, but they are supremely delicious!" Zola says. "So the papa of the young boy brought home a box of chocolate-covered cookies, and he proudly set them on the counter and went upstairs to wash."

"Uh-oh," I say, because I know this is not a good

thing. I can see what is coming. I have been around awhile.

Zola puts her hand out dramatically, as if she is stopping the wind. "Now the little boy knew not to touch the cookies. He knew that his papa would later open the box and allow each child to take precisely one cookie. Oh, Angel, how the boy longed for those cookies. He could hardly bear that he would have just one. He wished his father had never brought home the box at all. It was too awful to think of having to wait for the cookie, just one cookie, and that would be all."

At this point, Zola sighs and pauses, contipilating the sad situation. "Oh, Angel, the little boy snatched the box of cookies and fled to the basement and ate the cookies, all of them. He could not stop himself. They were so good, so perfectly delicious, so, so, *chocolate*."

"I knew it, Zola. I knew he would eat those cookies."

"Yes, Angel, yes. Later, the boy confessed, of course, because he was an honest boy, and he got a whipping."

"I was afraid of that, Zola."

"Yes, well. That is that. But now the boy is a man, and in his house he has a desk, and in his desk is one deep drawer, and in that one deep drawer he keeps mounds of chocolate: chocolate bars, chocolate candies, chocolate cookies! So many chocolates!"

"I understand this, Zola."

"Angel, any time of day or night he can select a chocolate something, but he does not make a pig of himself. Why do you think he keeps all those chocolates hidden in the drawer when he does not gobble them up?"

"Ah, Zola, ah. This I have seen! So many peoples have the secret drawers—or sometimes closets or boxes—and they have the little somethings in them. I am not talking about collections, like coins or knickle-knackles. I am talking about stashings of food or strange things—like Signor Rubini, you know him? The square man from up the hill?"

Zola presses her fingers to her lips. "The one who sits on the red bench, with his wool cap in one hand and his cane in the other?"

"Yes, yes, that's Signor Rubini. He has a secret drawer, and in it he has dozens and dozens of pairs of navy-blue socks! Is true. He cannot *wear* so many, but he *needs* so many because when he was a child he was always cold, especially his feet, and now he has the secret stash of socks for, for, how you say? For insurance, maybe?"

"Ah," Zola says. "Aha! Insurance!"

I had forgotten the chocolate-drawer story of Zola's until I see Mr. Pomodoro open a deep drawer in his desk, and inside, what do you think? Chocolates! Boxes of chocolate-covered cherries and chocolate-covered

almonds. Chocolate cookies and chocolate bars, stacks
of them. Mr. Pomodoro opens the drawer, gazes inside,
and removes one chocolate-covered cherry. He eats it
slowly.

I have already seen what Zola keeps in the top drawer
of her desk. She keeps rocks: jagged rocks, smooth rocks,
big rocks, little rocks. From time to time, she opens the
drawer, selects a rock, turns it around in her hands, studies it, and then returns it to the drawer. I feel as if she is
collecting pieces to make a mountain. Is this insurance?

Zola also has another secret drawer. In it, wrapped
in a piece of blue silk cloth, are feathers: mostly slenderly,
gray or white. I wonder about these feathers. What kind
of insurance do feathers offer?

MY TERRITORY

〜〜〜

W hat exactly is my territory? I don't have the information. Maybe it is the whole village, maybe
only part of the village, maybe one family, maybe one
person, but which one? Who is going to tell me? I am
never seeing other angels, not even when I float north
and visit the goats. Where are all the angels?

And how does Zola know what angels are supposed
to do? Why is she always telling me I'm supposed to
know this and that?

Today Zola says to me, "So, no swords?"

"What is sword?"

Zola slaps her headfore. "You must be a very young
angel."

This is making me mad. I am hundreds of years old,

and she is just a puny few-years-old people. Maybe ten. Maybe twelve. Maybe eight. *Puh!*

Zola says, "Angels used to fight, you know. They weren't always sweet and loving and peaceful."

She thinks *I* am "sweet and loving and peaceful"?

So Zola tells me a story about a fearsome battle between angels and evil beings. The angels rode flying white horses and slashed swords and threw thunderbolts. They were strong like warriors, and they defeated the evil beings in a long and mighty battle.

"Those were some amazing angels," Zola says. "Do you do anything like that?"

"Like what?"

"Like ride flying horses and slash swords and throw thunderbolts."

She isn't kidding. I can tell she really wants me to say yes, and I am even considering saying yes because then she will be impressified with me, but before I can answer her, she says, "Are angels dead people?"

"What? What? No! I am not a dead people. I am an angel! A people is a people and an angel is an angel!"

"Okay, okay," Zola says. "Take it easy." She runs a finger along the stone ledge, tracing a vein in the rock. Then, just when I am calming down, she says, "Are you a boy angel or a girl angel?"

"What?" I don't know why she is making me so

fidgetated. I am not used to peoples seeing me, and I am especially not used to peoples asking me questions. Usually the peoples who see me are the ones who are in great dangering or are very sickly. They smile on me. I make them peaceful.

Zola is studying me. "It's hard to tell. You could be a long-haired boy or a sturdy girl."

"I am an angel," I say. "I thought you knew a lot about angels. I am not a boy or a girl. I am angel. Angel. Angel!"

"Ah," Zola says, nodding, her chip-chop hair flicking up and down. "It's just that in churches, you know, sometimes the angels are women in long dresses, and sometimes they are babies, and—"

"Oh. Churches. I do not know about all those angels." This is something very confusing to me. Zola is right: Some are women and some are babies, and it is a puzzlement because never I see these angels in real, only in stone and in paintings. Do some angels look like this? Am I supposed to look like that? I ask Zola what I look like.

"What you *look* like?" she says. "Don't you know what you *look* like?"

"How would I know?" I say. "In a mirror I behold white fogness. Do I look like white fogness to you?"

"No, no," Zola says. She is studying me carefully

with the eyes with the large black poppils. "You look like—now don't get mad—you look like a person—"

"No! Not a people—"

"Well, wait, not exactly, no, no. You have the shape of a person, and a pleasing face—"

"Pleasing? Attractiful?"

"Yes, pleasing, I would say. The robe, hmm, is a bit long and crooked. . . ."

I hold out my arms. "It is?"

"Yes, but it's also sort of regal. You know what 'regal' is?"

"Of course, like king, like queen!"

Zola is trying to peer around behind me. "Where do the wings go?"

"Wings? What wings?"

Zola frowns. "Don't you have wings? I thought for sure, that first time I saw you, that you had wings."

I feel like I am going to bust into the tower walls and crimble into a thousand pieces. "I do not have wings." I say it slowly so that I do not sound too mad, but I am feeling hurt. "I am not a bird. I am an angel."

"Okay, okay, calm down," she says.

I am about to reassure her that I am perfectly calm when we hear *boom, boom, boom-de-boom, boom, boom, boom-de-boom.* It is Vinny on his drums. Then we hear *arf, arf, arf, arf, arf, arf, arf.*

Boom, boom, boom-de-boom—

Arf, arf, arf—

Zola leans over the balcony wall. "Be quiet! Shut up! Stop it! I'm going to kill you!"

If Zola had a thunderbolt, I think she would throw it.

Swishing in the Night

That night, after I check on the childrens in the chicken shad and beam them warm beams and see if they have found the figs I have left for them (they have), I wait until dark and then I flish into all the casas and apartamentos and sprinkle over the heads of all the sleeping adulterinos the knowingness of the hungry childrens. It takes a long time, but I am happy when I am done.

Now the peoples will do something, because peoples take care of other peoples, especially childrens, right?

I return to my hammock on the balcony just as the rosy headfore of morning begins to rise over the mountain. It is quiet, perfectly quiet, with only the sounds of mountains and trees humming.

POCKETA

Pocketa-pocketa-pocketa, pocketa-pocketa-pocketa, pocketa-pocketa-pocketa, pocketa-pocketa-pocket—

What is it? What is the awful *pocketa-pocketa-pocketa* noise?

Pocketa-pocketa-pocketa, pocketa-pocketa-pocketa—

It sounds like peoples playing that game, what is it, pong-ping? Like that, hitting the ball very fast back and forth, *pocketa-pocketa-pocketa.*

I flash here and there. Stop that noise! This is the peaceful village!

Pocketa-pocketa-pocketa—

Now *il beasto* joins in: *Arf, arf, arf, arf, arf, arf, arf, arf—*

Pocketa-pocketa—

It is a workman. He is in the old Pita building just down the road, and he is putting up walls for the school of Mr. Pomodoro. He has a new tool, an automatico nail driver. It goes like this: *Pocketa-pocketa-pocketa, pocketa-pocketa-pocketa—*

Signora Divino shouts out of her window. She tells the *pocketa* man to be quiet and then she says many ugly words. Next, Signor Rubini and then Signora Pompa and soon most of the villagers are leaning out of their windows with their ruffled bed hair and they are shouting ugly words at the *pocketa* man, who does not stop because he cannot hear them, what with all the *pocketa-pocketa-pocketa, pocketa-pocketa-pocketa.*

AGITATO

〜〜〜

There is no sleeping, no resting to be had with all the noise in the village. This used to be such a quiet place. You only would hear the birdies twirping and the church bells ringing.

I am a little crankiful when I am not sleeping well. I fling myself here and there on the balcony ledges, trying to knock myself into sleep. Then I give up and see over the scene. This is an intrigueful thing to do usually. You can see into everyone's yards and windows; you see them walking down the paths and lanes; you see the dogs chasing the cats chasing the mices; you see the birdies nesting and squabbling and flittering. There are always many things going on.

Today I see Zola's father, Mr. Pomodoro, on his

terrace, talking with an elderly man wearing painter's clothes. Mr. Pomodoro of the rubbery face has thick, black hair, and he has long bones with not much meat on them. He moves his arms a lot when he talks. The painter man stands very still, like a statue. It makes you want to poke him to see if he is alive.

Over there, to the right, I see Signora Mondopoco in her sheep boots. She is listening to two other women, who are speaking in a very *urgento* way.

Now Signora Divino comes out in her pink bedjacket over her black dress, and she throws a tub of dirty water on the bushes nearest our Casa Rosa, and then she goes to the back gate, where two old men and two old women are gathered. Signora Divino nods her head and then stamps her foot.

Something is up! Or down.

And then I remember that I did the flishing last night and the sprinkling over all the heads the knowingness of the hungry childrens. Aha! So this is good. Now they will do something to fix the hungry childrens.

Pretty soon, there are clomps of people in all the lanes and in the parco, and they are growing more *agitato*, waving their arms and stompling their feets. They are mad! Well, good. They *should* be mad that childrens are hungry and cold and all alone in the chicken shad.

And just when I am feeling mostest proud of my sprinkling work, Zola climbers up through the trippy-trap door and onto the balcony and says, "Angel! You have to *do* something!"

MAD PEOPLES

Zola, she is swooshing with her colorful skirts, three of them: red on top of green on top of blue; and two blouses, yellow over white; and violet leggings; and black ribbons in her hair and on her wrists. It is a smiling combination, and it makes me happy.

"Did you hear me?" Zola says. "You have to *do* something!"

I am not feeling too worried because I have already done the swishing in the night so that everyone will know about the hungry childrens.

"Angel! The people are mad!"

"Mad? Why?" If they are mad because the childrens are hungry, that is good, because if they are mad, they will do something.

"Because of the stealing, and now—"

"What stealing? What are you talking in my ears about?"

"The stealing—everyone is missing food and some are missing blankets and clothing. And I don't know how they found out about the children—"

"The childrens?" I say. "The childrens in the shad?"

Zola is *molto agitato*, kicking acorns all around the balcony. "Yes! So now they think the children are stealing from them and they called the police—"

"The police? The police are coming after the hungry childrens?"

"Yes," Zola says. "Angel! You have to *do* something!"

I do not feel so good.

Pocketa-pocketa-pocketa—

Arf, arf, arf—

Zola shouts over the edge of the balcony. "Be quiet!"

Mr. Pomodoro shouts from the terrace, "Be quiet!"

Pocketa-pocketa-pocketa—

Arf, arf, arf—

Signora Divino is gathering slugs in her garden. Her grandson, Vinny, is throwing a frog in the air. Signora Mondopoco is peeking inside her sheep boots. "Baa," she says fondly. "Baa, baa, baa."

How am I supposed to think with all this craziness going on?

"Angel!" Zola says.

"I know, I know. I will do something." And then I think, *Wait a minute. I do not have to do what Zola says! She is a people and I am an angel!*

Zola looks at me so pleading and begging. "Do something, Angel, please, I *beseech* you!"

Beseech? "Hokay, hokay, I will do something, but it will be what I *choose* to do."

Peoples! Why so bossy?

WHERE ARE PARENTS?

I have to think. I do not have the instant answers. While I am thinking of what to do about the police going after the hungry childrens, I am wondering where are the parents of the childrens? Why are they all alone, with only other childrens for company? And while I am wondering this, I also think about Zola.

Where is *her* mother? I want to ask, but it seems too bold, no? She wants me to do this; she wants me to do that. Why can't I ask her a little question?

Pocketa-pocketa-pocketa—

Arf, arf, arf—

"Be quiet, you annoying arfing dog!"

Arf, arf, arf—

Zola scrabbles up a handful of acorns and tosses them

over the side of the balcony. "You most annoying dog in the universe!" Now she unties a ribbon from her ankle and wraps it loosely at her neckle.

Boom, boom, boom-de-boom—

"Auf!" Zola says. "The drums of Vinny!"

Boom, boom—

Arf, arf, arf—

"Be quiet, you artichoke!" And then Zola turns to me and says, "Where is Vinny's mother? And father? How come he lives with his grandmother?"

"That is a twisty tale," I say. "I will tell you later, because now I have to swish the heads of the childrens." I float off the balcony, but then I turn back, full of nosy courage. "Zola! Where is *your* mother? And do you have a brother? And why do you live with your father?"

Zola pinches her lips as if she has sucked on a peppercorn. "A mother, a brother, a father?" She turns that into a tune: "A moth-er, a broth-er, a fath-er. A doodle, a dandle, a candle." She disappears through the trippy-trap door, just like that.

INSIDE THE MOUNTAINS

All around are the mountains. I used to think the mountains were made of dirt: heaps of dirt piled high. Now I know they are mostly rock with dirt on top. I mentioned this to Zola one day and she said, "Of *course* the mountains are rock," and then she gave me the scowl that tells me I am *stupido*.

An angel is *not stupido*!

What I like is that the houses and the churches and the paths and steps and walls and towers in this village are all made from the rock of the mountains, so the inside of the mountain is on the outside. And the houses made of rock and stone, they are like childrens of the mountain sprinkled all around, close by. That gives me a good feeling.

On the inside of the mountains, where the rock for the houses and the roads and churches and towers used to be, is the secret that everyone who lives here knows. Inside the mountains is dynamite to blow up bridges to keep out invaders, and inside the mountains are airplanes ready to zoom into the air in a blink to keep out invaders. Inside the mountains are food and guns and ammunition and water and blankets and medical equipment. Inside some mountains it is like a whole village. I am not kidding you.

All of the peoples here know this and they know where to go if the invaders come and they know what is their job to protect their country. Sometimes I think that is extramarkable and smart, and sometimes I think it is so sadful that peoples have to worry about invaders. Why would peoples invade other peoples? Don't they know the other peoples are like their own peoples, who don't want to be invaded? I get *agitato* if I think about it too much.

What calms me down is the rock of the houses and the towers and the churches. The rock is so strong and has been here forever and will still be here even if peoples make a mashmish of things. The rock of the tower makes me feel safe.

I hurry to swish to the hungry childrens, who are not

in the shad because they have heard that the police are coming, and so they are hiding here, there, and there. I flish into their heads to let them know where to go. To the rock. To the tower. My tower.

PERMISSIONS

I don't need the permission of Zola or Mr. Pomodoro, but I think it is better to have at least Zola in the knowing. It is funny about peoples, but they like to be in the knowing; they like to give permissions; they do not so much like surprisements unless the surprisement is a lot of gold dropped into their laps.

So I tell Zola the childrens are coming. They will enter through the basement doorway and make their way up the back steps to the lower tower rooms. This way they do not have to go through the house and they will not frighten Mr. Pomodoro.

Zola says, "He won't like it. He'll say he needs permission from the authorities—the police or whoever would be in charge of the children."

"I am thinking no one is in charge of the childrens, or else they would not be hungry and cold in the chicken shad."

"No, I mean *officially*. So we don't get in trouble."

"In trouble for what?"

"For hiding the children."

"We are not hiding. We are protecting."

Zola is kicking the acorns again. "Okay, then," she says. "Okay. Let's see what happens. Let's see if the children will be quiet." She does the smile with her mouth and I think maybe she likes this plan.

The police are out hunting for the childrens, but the childrens have managed to hide themselves well, and as soon as it is dark they slip into the tower one by two by one. Zola brings blankets and pillows and bread and cheese and chocolate. She adds three stuffed animals and extra socks and scarves and some of her swirly skirts and ribbons.

The childrens are surprised by what they see, and at first they are suspicious. They think it is a trip-trap. Zola tries to explain to them that they are safe, but they are not understanding her words, so I flish inside their heads to calm them.

WHAT IT MEANS?

Here in the Ticino, in the south of Switzerland, the peoples mostly speak Italian. In another part of Switzerland, the Swiss peoples speak French; in another part German; and yet another tiny part Romansch. But the Swiss peoples are so smart that most of them can speak all those languages and switch from one to another zoomzoomzoom just like that and *then* they will dizzy you and switch to English. How they are holding all those words in their heads?

Many tourists come to this part of Switzerland, but most of the tourists are stubborn and only want to speak their own language, very loudly. They will inspect a menu and then say to the waiter (in English or Swedish or Japanese): "What it means? WHAT IT MEANS?"

The Swiss people are used to this. They don't swat the tourists on the heads with the menus. Mostly they don't say rude words or spit on the ground. No, they smile politely and manage to explain calmly, either in the tourist's language or by an incredilish movement of their hands, what it means.

This impressifies me.

When Mr. Pomodoro goes into the pharmacy hoping to find some nasal spray and asks for *puzzo di naso*, the Italian-speaking clerk does not fall in the aisle laughing because Mr. Pomodoro has asked for "nose stinky." No, the kindiful clerk does not even feel the need to correct Mr. Pomodoro; instead the clerk smiles politely and reaches for a bottle of *spruzzo* (not *puzzo*) *di naso*. Maybe the clerk will laugh after Mr. Pomodoro leaves, but she will not laugh in front of the person who does not have the right words.

I loaf this. I loaf it very much.

In the tower, with the hungry childrens, I am wishing I had some of these Swiss peoples with all the words. Zola and I are trying to understand what the childrens are saying. They speak very fast, zoomzoomzoom, so fast the words fly out of their mouths and disappear into the air before you can catch them with your own ears.

I tell Zola she will have to do the talking. The childrens won't be able to see me, and they might be frightened if Zola talks to an invisible someone. They will think it is a ghost. Or that she is kookoo. Only one young boy seems to sense my presence. He stands near me and stares and blinks his eyes as if the light is too bright, but it is dark in the tower room beneath the balcony, with only the starlight and moonlight outside the small window.

This boy puts his hands forward as if he is parting the air. "Wow," he whispers. He stands on my robe. This is hokay; many times peoples have stood on me. Animals, too. They do not know what they are doing. It does not hurt.

There are three girls and five boys. The youngest, who is maybe five, is the "wow" boy; the oldest is a boy about ten or eleven. Most speak a little English. They are all dirty, from head to foot, and dressed in odd combinations of old clothes and newer ones, and in clothes too small or too large. I recognize, on one girl's head, an old scarf of Signora Mondopoco. The youngest boy wears the weathered hat of Signora Divino's deadened husband.

The childrens are not related to each other and do not all speak the same language. They are straggled together, maybe from an orphanage in another country. It is hardness to understand everything that is jumping out of their mouths.

In quiet voicing, Zola asks each one's name. I loaf this, that she does not treat them like a herd of sheep.

She wants to study each face and say a name. The boys are Paolo, Manuel, Stefan, Franz, and Josef. The girls are Terese, Rosetta, and Nicola. Zola hears each name once and does not forget it.

Once we know their names, we start to see their peoplealities. The youngest one, Josef, is all eyeballs and interest. He says "Wow!" and "*Was ist das?*" The smallest girl, Nicola, says, about once an hour, "Be *nice* to me! Be *nice* to me!" Rosetta is so quiet, always glancing down shyly, her hand clutching a torn piece of cloth which she occasionally rubs against her cheek.

Franz is maybe a little confused. If anyone speaks to him, he repeats, "*Glocken, glocken, glocken.*" I think this means "bells, bells, bells," and I do not know why he is saying this. The other childrens don't seem to find this odd, though.

Terese is impressified with Zola and imitates the way Zola stands, the way she holds her head and moves her arms. It is not a mocking way. It is as if Terese is trying out what it would be like to *be* Zola.

Then there is Stefan. He does not say much but clomps around making strange faces and noises, to make the others laugh. They do laugh at him sometimes, but Stefan is the one with the saddest eyes of all.

Manuel is jumpy, like a hot bean. Noises, moths, shadows, all these things stiffen his arms and shoulders and even his hair, if you can find this believing. Lastly, there is Paolo, the oldest boy, who is maybe Zola's age. He has a smart head and a watching eye.

Zola says to Paolo: "Tell them we will bring food."

"Who is 'we'?" Paolo asks.

"Um. Me and a . . . a . . . helper."

Helper? Now I am the *helper* of Zola?

"Tell them," Zola says, "not to steal anymore. They could get in trouble. We will try to get them what they need. No stealing. Stealing is bad. Okay?"

Paolo zips into a swirl of words in the languages of the childrens. Then, to be sure everyone understands, he acts out sneaking around and stealing something; he pretends to eat the something. Then he shouts "No! *Molto* bad! No!" and he chops himself in the head and falls onto the ground. "Bad!"

Stefan thinks this is a game. He pretends to grab something and then clonks himself in the head and falls onto the ground. "Bad! Bad!"

Terese laughs; Rosetta cries; Nicola says, "Be *nice* to me!"; the rest look puzzled.

It is going to be a long, long night.

WHAT IS TIME?

Peoples, why are they so compelsive, no, what is the word, propulsive, no, obsessive, yes obsessive! Why they are so obsessive about time, and why they think it is like a cake you can divide into pieces, why? Why they have to have seconds, pinutes, hours, days, weeks, months, years, decades, sentries, on and on, tick-tick, whoosh there goes two seconds, whoosh, two more. What, they are thinking time is going somewhere? Where it is going, I ask you, where?

Listen. You hear any ticking? No. You hear just the world being the world. You see any clocks in the sky? You see calendars on the trees?

Zola, she keeps asking me time questions, like: How

long will the childrens stay in the tower? How long will the childrens sleep? What will they do when morning comes? How many hours, how many pinutes, what time, when, *ack, ack ack*!

Hokay. Hokay. I am calmed down now. Hokay.

This was a problem last night: Childrens have to go to the toilet. Goodly, there is a toilet in the basement, but still they have to go up and down the narrow creaky stairs to get to the toilet and when you flosh the toilet it makes a noise like a frog burping. So all night long there was *creak, creak, crickle, creak, BURPLE BURP, creak, creak, crickle, creak.* Then a tiny quiet. Then *creak, creak, crickle, creak, BURPLE BURP, creak, creak, crickle.*

And whenever I hear the creaks and the burples I am fearing that Mr. Pomodoro will wake up and think there is a burglar in the house, and what if he has a gun and tries to shoot the burglar who isn't really a burglar but is a children going to the toilet? So all night long, I am going up and down the creaking stairs with the childrens to protect them.

Maybe peoples will tell you that the night has eight hours or seven hours or wentever, but I tell you there are long nights and short nights, not same-number-hours nights, and this night was a very, very, very, very long night. Goodly, though, Mr. Pomodoro did not wake up. Neither did Zola, which I found a tiny bit annoying because wasn't *she* the one so worried about the hungry childrens?

When I am finally draping myself in the gauzy hammock on the balcony, and the pink headfore of sun is peeking over the mountain, Zola bounds up through the trippy-trap doors and into the rooms below bringing bread and cheese, and then she zips up to the balcony. She is wearing three dresses: blue over pink over white, and green socks and green shoes and six or nineteen ribbons in her hair. It looks more attracting than you might think.

The childrens snore on. They don't even wake up for the food or for more creaking to the toilet. They are tired from all that down and up the stairs all night.

"Angel!" Zola says. "We've got to get busy!"

"What? What are you talking about?"

"Are we telling anyone about the children? And then what? What if someone takes them away to an orphanage? That's where they were, Paolo says. A bad orphanage. But not in this country. And then they lived in ditches. Ditches! What's the plan?"

"Plan?" She is expecting *me* to have a plan?

"What's next?"

"Next?"

"Angel! Are you having a hearing problem?"

And she goes on, "When should . . ." and "What time will . . ." and myself is woozy sleepy and I want to go lie down in the pasture of the goats.

PARADISE

~~~~~~~~~~~~~~~~~~~~

"Behold," I say to Zola. "Behold the sky, pinking with morning. Behold the soft white moon going to sleep now. Behold the blue mountains, so tall, all around us, with the white snow far up on the tops. Behold the green trees and the yellowy stone houses and the rock paths terracing up the mountainsides. Take a big bulp of air. Ahhh. Behold the towers of the churches. Behold the lake down there at the feets of the mountains, so green and silver, so still. Take another big bulp of air. Ahhh."

Zola is leaning against the balcony wall, smalling—what is that word again?—oh, smiling! Zola is smiling at the paradise around us.

"Zola, peoples is running around like chickens and they forget that—"

Pocketa-pocketa-pocketa—

"Eww," Zola says. "What is that noise?"

"It is the noise of the wall-making man at the school of Pomodoro. Wait! Wait!"

"What?"

"That's it! The hungry childrens will go to the school of Pomodoro, and—childrens can live at the school, right?"

"Well, older children can—he wasn't planning on having young children boarding there, and besides—"

"No besides! Is perfect! Perfect!"

"But—"

"No butting! Is perfect!"

"Angel! He is going to find a lot of reasons why the children would not be able to go to the school."

"How many childrens he has already enrolled in this school?"

Zola studies the snow on the far mountains. "I couldn't say for sure."

"Guess. Appiximately. A hundred? Two hundred? Seven hundred?"

"I don't have the exact figures—"

"Appiximate! I am trying to understand if there is space for the childrens."

"Well, there aren't actually confirmed enrollments for everyone yet."

"Zola, for how many is there the confirming?"

"Let me see. There might be, I think, maybe four."

"Four hundred students? And how many beds?"

"No, four students. Four."

"Four?"

THE NATURE OF PAPAS

Papas especially do not usually like surprisements, unless it is the gold falling in the laps or the horses winning the races. Papas can react very badly to surprisements, this I have seen, like when Signora Divino's husband was a papa and his son said, "Papa, the car went into the lake." This was a surprisement that Papa Divino did not like and he went very much loudly crazy.

Usually the mamas are standing there saying, "Now, now, let's calm down, shh, shh, no need to throw the chair out the window, shh," which is what Signora Divino often found herself saying. And when the papas do calm down, the strange thing is they are very soft in the heart and they are just glad their childrens are alive and well.

When Zola goes to get Mr. Pomodoro to show him

the childrens, I am thinking maybe we should have pre-
pared him first. This will not be a good surprisement,
and where is the mama to calm him down?

But here is the funny thing that happens: Zola leads
Mr. Pomodoro into the first tower room, where all of
the childrens have gathered to eat the bread and cheese.
As soon as Mr. Pomodoro enters the room, Josef, the
little wow-boy, runs to him and grabs his knees and says,
"Papa! Papa! Papa!" and then shy Rosetta runs to him
and does the same, and the rest of the childrens gaze at
Mr. Pomodoro with big, round eyes, very black, like the
eyes of kindly puppies.

And Mr. Pomodoro does not throw a chair out the
window or anything like that. Instead, he stands there
with the childrens hugging his knees and he weeps. Just
a little bit. And very quietly.

THE NATURE OF
SIGNORA DIVINO

Now it is true that Signora Divino and her grandson, Vinny, sometimes make me want to throw pinecones or to pinch them slightly, but I need to tell you more so you will understand why I watch over them.

I am there when Signora Divino is born. I am summoned because she is stuck inside her mama. It takes a lot of flishing here and there and much calming of the air and the midwives, but at last the baby is delivered. Her name is Marianna DiPuccio. Her lips curl up at the sides in a friendly way and her wee mouth is puckered as if to give a kiss or make a bubble. I like this little baby and I stick around to be sure she is hokay.

Such a funny child, like she will ask a tree if she can

borrow a twig, and she will burst into song in the middle of church, and she will tell you everything you might want to know about fairies or dinosaurs. Sometimes she is an impish child, too, sneaking chocolates and bringing worms into the house. I like to be in her energy. So much laughing and goodwill.

I am there for her wedding to Signor Divino and when their son, Massimo, is born and while he is growing up and losing the car in the lake and taking flying lessons and many things like that. And I am there when the son marries Bette and when they have a son, Vinny. Signora Divino is so happy to have a grandson.

And one day, a day of blue sky and spring breezes, Massimo tells his mama and papa to sit on the terrace with Vinny and watch the sky and maybe in an hour or so they will see something beautiful. And so Signor and Signora Divino and their two-year-old grandson, Vinny, sit on the terrace in the afternoon sun and they enjoy the air on their faces and they watch the sky.

They hear a humming sound, the drone of a small plane, and they turn as the plane enters the valley between the mountains. Vinny claps his hands. He loves planes.

And then Signora Divino knows. "It's Massimo!" She waves elaborately. She sees the yellow scarf of Bette, Massimo's wife. "Look, Vinny! It's your mama and papa!"

The plane flies lower and dips its wings toward the house of the Divinos. Oh, it is exciting to see! Signora Divino calls to the neighbors. "Come, come, look! It's Massimo!"

The plane soars to the end of the valley, rises and turns elegantly, heading back toward the local airport to the west. Such a day! Such blue sky and purple mountains so sturdy and silver lake so calm and still. Such a day!

And then *bip-bip,* an odd noise, a stuttering *bip-a-bip-bip* and a narrow plume of white smoke and a loud banging and the jerking of the plane and Signor and Signora Divino and their friends shouting, "No, no, no!" and little Vinny clapping his hands.

Bip-a-bip-bip whirrrr. The plane regains its course and dips over the mountain as everyone strains to see and listen. Is the plane in good form? Will it crash? Will it make it to the airport?

All they hear is a low drone.

"Is normal?" Signor Divino asks no one in particular. "Is good?"

Signora Divino slumps into a chair and remains like a flour sack, limp, mute.

Signor Divino and a neighbor race to the airport. An hour later they return with the triumphant Massimo and Bette.

"Whew!" Massimo says. "Whew! There must have been an angel watching over us!"

Ho boy! Not just "watching," but flishing and flailing and swirling the air currents!

"Papa, Papa!" Vinny says.

Massimo sees his mother, aflump in the chair. "Mama?" Massimo says. "Mama?"

Signora Divino cannot speak. The shock has been too much. For two weeks she does not speak. When she hears the drone of a plane outside, she covers her ears and crouches.

And then one day, she speaks. "I make ravioli," is what she says, and on she goes, but she is not the same. She seems hard on the outside, but inside is soft and fragile like an egg. When her husband dies later that year, the outside gets harder and the inside softer.

Now her son, Massimo, and his wife, Bette, are in America for three months. They are thinking of moving there, to Virginia, where Bette's sister lives. Her sister wants to open a school, an international school. Signora Divino thinks this is crazy idea.

And now Mr. Pomodoro says he is opening an international school right here, in Switzerland, and she thinks the whole world is looloo. Why can't Mr. Pomodoro go home and Massimo and Bette come back and open their school here, so Vinny and Massimo and Bette could stay close by and Signora Divino would not be alone? Why?

I protect the Signora if I can. If I pinch her and Vinny or throw pinecones, it is only because I do not want them to become crooked and bitter. I want them to remember what it is like to think, "Such a day!"

A BIGGA MESS

~~~

S o, we have the childrens from the chicken shad in
the tower, clinging to Mr. Pomodoro's knees, and he
sees their big black soft puppyful eyes, and little Josef is
saying, "Papa! Papa!" and outside is the *pocketa-pocketa-
pocketa* and the *arf, arf, arf, arf, arf*.

Mr. Pomodoro does his best. He goes in search of the
mayor of the *commune*, but the mayor is in the Canary
Islands on holiday, so then Mr. Pomodoro searches for
the vice mayor, but he is away at his fishing cabin, and
so round and round Mr. Pomodoro goes, trying to find
someone to give the permission to sort out the childrens.

The police decide it is their job, and they want the
passports of the childrens, but of course the childrens
are not walking around with passports. They don't know

what the policeman is talking about.

"We don't have any credit cards," Paolo says.

"Not credit cards, passports. PASS. PORTS."

The childrens shrug.

The policeman thinks the childrens should come to the police station, but the childrens start crying and shouting, "Papa, Papa!" and outside is the noise, the *pocketa-pocketa-pocketa* and the *arf, arf, arf,* and the policeman tells Zola's father, hokay, he can look after the childrens until something official is sorted out.

"And when might that be?" Mr. Pomodoro asks.

The policeman looks at the crowded tower room and the dirty childrens and he hears the noise outside and inside and he says, "I don't know. It's a bigga mess."

THE DRUMS

The childrens are taking turns up and down the creaky stairs to bathe in the big tub and to wash their hairs. Much water is dripping.

Mr. Pomodoro goes zoomzoom down to the Migros by the airport to buy eight pairs of jeans, eight shirts and sweaters, and eight pairs of socks and underwear, all in the same colors so no one will be fighting. Rosetta and Terese do not want to wear the jeans; they want to wear Zola's swirly skirts.

Signora Divino knocks on the door of Casa Rosa. Zola shouts up to Mr. Pomodoro. "It's Signora Divino. She wants her hair."

"Her what?"

"Her hair."

Paolo is summoned to translate. "Her *hat*," he says. "She wants her *hat*. She says the bad children stole it." He turns back to Signora Divino and says something in Italian and then he stamps his foot and goes upstairs and returns with the hat of Signora Divino's deadened husband.

Later that day, Mr. Pomodoro leads the clean childrens in their clean clothes through the village, stopping at various casas along the way.

"Signora Mondopoco? Your scarf, I believe?" Mr. Pomodoro's long, wibbly arm nudges Terese forward. When Terese offers the scarf, Signora Mondopoco smiles broadly and clasps her scarf as if it is a lovely, new present.

"*Grazie*," Signora Mondopoco says. "*Molto grazie!*" And then she returns the scarf to Terese, draping it on her neck, and says, "*Molto* better, *sì*? *Molto* better." The Signora waves good-bye.

Two people are not so friendly. Signora Pompa roughly snatches a sweater back from Nicola. Nicola stomps her foot and says, "Be *nice* to me!" When Franz reluctantly returns a leather pouch to Signor Rubini, Signor Rubini says, "Bad! Bad! Bad!" Franz interrupts with, "*Glocken, glocken, glocken.*" Signor Rubini slams his door.

As Zola, Mr. Pomodoro, and the childrens return to Casa Rosa, they hear *boom, boom, boom-de-boom*—

Zola puts her hands to her head. "Auf . . ."

Paolo alertens to the sound and runs to the gate of the Divinos. Vinny is drumming like the *pocketa* man, very fast *pocketa-boom, pocketa-boom, pocketa-boom-boom-boom.*

Josef says, "Wow! *Was ist das?*" and he, too, runs to the gate of the Divinos. Soon all the childrens are gathered round, and when Vinny realizes he has an audience, he goes faster and faster with the wooden sticks, what you call them? Drumsticks? Is that not chicken legs?

Faster and faster Vinny goes, and the childrens clap. They say, "Bravo! Bravo!"

And you can see Vinny's cheeks with their pinkness of pride and you can see Signora Divino peeking out of the kitchen window almost shyly.

RAVIOLI

At night I flish some more in the heads of the sleeping villagers. It is not much I am doing. Mostly I am sprinkling images of the hungry childrens with the puppy eyes. Sometimes, hokay, I admit, sometimes I also sprinkle soft sounds, like the childrens saying very softly, "Papa, Papa," and "Mama, Mama," and "Nonna" and "Nonno." But that is all. I do not want to intrude too much.

The next day, around noon, Signora Divino knocks at the door of Casa Rosa. Zola opens the door and, suspicious, peers around the Signora to see if she has brought snakes or slugs with her.

Signora Divino says, "I make ravioli. *Andiamo, andiamo!* Let's go!" She turns toward her house. "For the *bambini*, the *ragazzi*, ravioli! *Andiamo!*"

And so all of the childrens, along with Zola and Mr. Pomodoro, file into the kitchen of Signora Divino, where Vinny is setting plates on the table.

Zola says, "What are *you* smiling about?"

"Ravioli."

As soon as the childrens start eating, Vinny begins playing his drums. *Boom, boom, boom-de-boom, boom-diddy-boom-diddy-boom-boom-boom.*

Signora Divino beams. "Entertainment."

Boom, boom, boom-de-boom, boom-diddy-boom-diddy-boom-boom-boom.

At the end of the meal, when the childrens have eaten every last ravioli and mopped the sauce from their plates with their bread, they turn their black doggy eyes on Signora Divino.

"Hokay, hokay," she says. "Tomorrow, ravioli. *Ancora.* Again!"

Little Nicola whispers "ravioli" with reverence. "Ravioli, ravioli."

"*Ecco,*" says Signora Divino. "I need to know one thing. Who is the one who took the hat of my dead husband?"

The childrens stare down at their feets, ashamed. It is quiet in the room.

"Tell me."

Josef stands up. "I sorry. I did it. Head cold, hat warm."

Signora Divino leaves the room, returning moments later with the hat in her hand. She places the hat on Josef's head. "*Ecco,*" she says. "Is better on your head. My dead husband no need a hat."

And then, because the childrens are a little greedy, it is true, Paolo says, "Is there anything else your dead husband doesn't need?"

Signora Divino gasps and covers her mouth with her hand. Then, boops, she laughs, a modest laugh that gets bigger and bigger and soon everyone is laughing.

Signora Divino says, "I will have an inspection. I will let you know. Now go away. I need a resting. And remember, tomorrow—ravioli!"

MEATBALLS

In the village live mostly old peoples. Why this is, is puzzlement. There used to be few houses and many childrens; now there are many houses and few childrens. The young families, they are urgent to go to big cities or to other countries. *It will be perfecto there!* they think. *We will be rich!* and *We will have big house! Big car! Big boat!*

Sometimes the young men and women go because their parents are driving them crazy. *We will be free!* and *We can do whatever we want!*

And so off they go, the young men and women and the young families and the little *bambini*, leaving the old peoples behind to bend for themselves. They leave behind the beautiful mountains, the lakes, the clear air and blue skies and the sheep and the goats.

And after the young men and women and families have been in their new cities or lands for some short while, they wake up in the night sometimes and they miss the mountains and lakes and air and skies and sheep and goats. They miss the old peoples.

Why am I telling you this today? Because all night long I was tending the old peoples: Signora Mondopoco, of the sheep boots, who felt a heavy goat on her chest; and Signor Rubini, with his drawer full of socks, who could not sleep—so much he was missing his son and his grandchildrens off in America; and Signora Pompa, who was calling out in the night for her daughter who lives in Paris. When finally I return to my tower, I fall asleep in the hammock and hear nothing until the church bells at noon. Noon! Lazy head!

I discover Zola and Mr. Pomodoro and the childrens at the casa of Signora Divino. They have eaten more ravioli, and now they are entering the alley behind her house. There they find a dozen villagers seated in plastic chairs behind a long table. How funny they look, all lined up like that, as if they are at a fly market.

On the table is a mishmasheroni: hats, scarves, gloves, socks, meatballs, chocolate cake, a lightflash, cro-cheted slippers, a fishing rod, bars of chocolate, cuddle animals, dolls, a music box, necklaces, a figurine, soccer balls, a drawing tablet, coal pencils, an easel, yarn, and rice pudding.

The villagers are smiling proudly, their hands clasped neatly in their laps.

"*Ecco*," Signora Divino says, wivvling her arm over the bounty on the table. "*Ecco.*"

"What are we supposed to do?" Paolo asks.

Manuel, the jumpy boy, says, "It's a testo. They want to see if we will steal, and then if we do, they will shoot us."

Nicola whimpers. "No shooting! Please!"

Signora Divino says, "No, no, no shooting. Is for you . . ." Again she wivvles her arm over the meatballs and soccer balls and dolls and hats. "Is freely! Freely!"

Still the childrens hang back. They are not trusting.

Mr. Pomodoro leads the quietest child, Rosetta, to the table. "What would you like to have?"

Rosetta lowers her head, tucking her chin into her neck. "*Niente.*"

"Nothing? Surely there is something here—what about a necklace? Hmm? Or a scarf?"

Rosetta tilts her head to one side, her chin still safely tucked into her neck. "*Cavallo?*" she says softly.

"No!" Stefan says. "Is trick! They shoot you!"

Rosetta's lips tremble as she ducks behind Mr. Pomodoro.

Little Nicola crouches behind Zola. "No shooting! Be nice!"

Mr. Pomodoro turns to Signora Divino for help. "What did Rosetta say? What's *cavallo*?"

"Ah, *bella, bella*," the Signora says, reaching across the table for one of the cuddle animals. "Horse—*cavallo—sì*?"

Rosetta beams and reaches up to touch the horse.

"Bang!" shouts Stefan. "Bang! Bang!"

Rosetta snatches the horse and whackles Stefan on the arm with it.

Franz is standing at one end of the table, eyeing a soccer ball. He taps his fingers on the table. *"Glocken, glocken, glocken."* Tentatively, his fingers crawl toward the soccer ball.

At the other end of the table, Terese's fingers are creeping toward the rice pudding.

And then, as if a signal has gone off that only the childrens can hear, all of their hands are reaching and grabbling and snatching. Manuel and Paolo are fighting over the meatballs, until Manuel overtakes and shoves them in his mouth.

"No, no!" says Signora Divino.

Nicola snatches the chocolate cake and gobbles it.

"No, no!"

Franz grabs the soccer ball and hugs it possessively.

Stefan and Josef battle for the fishing rod.

"No, no!"

Zola and her father and the villagers are watching with their mouths widely open, as if they are thinking, *What creatures are these?*

Finally Signora Divino manages to explaterate that everyone will have a chance, that there are plenty of meatballs and cake and pudding for all, and that other things can be shared, and really they must all stop fighting right this minute.

Signora Divino suggests that the villagers form a committee and find a better way to give things to the childrens. The villagers will try again *domani*, tomorrow.

"*Domani? Domani? No, no, oggi!* Today!" Paolo insists.

"*Sì, sì, oggi!*" chime in the others.

Even those who don't speak Italian take up the chant: "*Oggi! Oggi! Oggi!* Today! Today! Today!"

The villagers look a little bit frightened.

THE NATURE OF ZOLA

Zola, she is intrigueful to me. In her many-layered clothings, with her chippy-choppy hair and the eyes with the big black poppils, in her sometimes bossy way, she has also the soft heart of a bunny. The soft heart is also a smart heart because it is not soft for every puny silly thing, but over the things that are matterful. Are you knowing what I am meaning?

Today she clabbers up onto my balcony and says, "Angel! You have to *do* something!"

She is always telling me this. "What is it now?"

I know that the hungry childrens are not hungry today, and at night they no longer sleep in the tower rooms, but instead they have beds in the other rooms of Casa Rosa. I know that this morning Franz and Rosetta

walked Signora Pompa's dog and even scooped the dog
poop. I know that Terese and Manuel helped Signor
Rubini stir the rice pudding, and Paolo and Stefan
clumped meatballs with Signora Divino. Below, I see
Nicola and Josef kicking a soccer ball.

"Angel!"

"Zola, is it about the childrens?"

"No," she says. "It is Signora Mondopoco."

Signora Mondopoco is the old woman with the sheep
boots.

"You have to do something!" Zola repeats. "She's very
old and she thinks she is going to die!"

"This I know."

"Well, what are you going to *do*, Angel?"

I do not know what to say to Zola. Very old peoples
do die. Their bodies have the parts that stop working and
fall off, no, not fall off but fall—how do you say? Apart?
They fall apart. It is hard to keep going on when your
body is clunking away.

"Angel!"

"Zola, you know what Signora Mondopoco likes?
She likes poppets."

"Poppets?"

"Little dollies. You have any little dollies?"

"No. I'm too big for dollies."

"Oh. Well, Signora Mondopoco is very big and she

loves dollies. She is like a little girl in her mind sometimes."

Zola thinks about this, and then she goes away and later that day she brings to me a poppet dolly that she has made out of a dish towel and many colored ribbons. It is a sweet little doll but it has no face.

"Zola, maybe you could give the dolly some eyes and a nose and mouth."

"Oh, right."

So Zola goes away and returns later with the dolly that now has large round blue eyes with fluttery black lashes, a pink smalling mouth, and spots on her cheeks.

"She has the measlies?"

"Those are *freckles,* Angel. *Freckles.*"

"No nose?"

"I couldn't do a nose."

Zola takes the dolly to Signora Mondopoco, who is so happy to meet the dolly. Really, really happy. She claps her hands. Then she pulls from her pocket a worn and smudged wee dolly and introduces the worn dolly to the new dolly. Signora Mondopoco uses doll voices:

"Ciao!"

"Ciao!"

She carries on in Italian, but what she is saying is, "I am happy to meet you" and "Me too!" and "Will you live with me?" and "Do you snore?" and "Only a little." It is not a very advanced conversation, but it is one that makes Signora Mondopoco very happy.

Later, Zola says to me in a sober way, "I like that Signora Mondopoco. I like her very much." In Zola's palm is a small granite rock, which she balances on the stone wall. "I hope that when I get old, someone will make a dolly for me."

TRANSPORT

Today is Sunday and throughout the valley the church bells are pealing *dong dong la-dong*, that most warming of sounds ringing in the air, *dong dong la-dong*. The childrens in Casa Rosa are beginning to wake up, Mr. Pomodoro is making pancakes, and Zola is— where is Zola? Somewhere out and about already.

Signora Divino, I see her in her yard in her pink bedjacket, gazing up at the mountains and listening to the bells. Vinny is in the kitchen, stirring hot chocolate. Soon one of the villagers will come to the gate of Signora Divino and give her the news about Signora Mondopoco.

Last night when I visited Signora Mondopoco, she was in her bed, draped with a soft blanket, her hands gently crossed on her chest. Beneath her hands she protected her worn dolly and her new dolly. She closed her eyes and said, "I am ready, dollies."

On her rooftop I placed a sleeping frog. When it woke and made its croaky sound, the transport angel would come. I was going to stay and wait and ask the transport angel all my questions, but it did not seem right to interrupt the flight of Signora Mondopoco.

And so I returned to my hammock on the balcony and just as the pink headfore of morning rose above the mountain, I heard the frog speak and I saw, in an instant, the golden light surround the casa of Signora Mondopoco. Sometimes when the sun is directly overhead and shines onto the lake, the light is so bright it pickles your eyes and you have to turn away from it. But the golden light is different; it becomes paler and paler so that you have to strain to see it, and you wish your eyeballs were bigger, and then, then, it is gone.

WHAT ZOLA KNOWS

Zola clops up to the balcony and collapses in the hammock. "Oh, Angel!" she says. "How can you bear it?"

"Bear what?"

"Signora Mondopoco is gone. Did you visit her? How can you bear it, to see them go?"

"Well, it is peoples, you know. Peoples are not going to live a million years."

"Well, then, what am I supposed to be *doing*?"

Zola. There she is in her violet dress over the green skirt over the yellow skirt, bare feet, orange ribbons around her ankles and in her chippy-choppy hair. Between two fingers she holds a slenderly gray feather.

"I don't know, Zola. Peoples find ways, they find things, interests, you will find . . ." I am all tangled up with the words.

"But *I* am not a peoples," Zola says.

"What?"

"I am not a peoples."

"What?" My head, I think, has come off and is jumping in the trees. "But you have a papa—Mr. Pomodoro. . . ."

Zola lazily swings a foot over the side of the hammock. "He is not my papa. I am not a peoples."

"What?" I think my head is now my foot and my foot is my head. "But the peoples—they can see you."

"Yes," she says, scratching a scab on her knee. "Why *is* that?"

"But—but—ha! You cannot float or flish."

"Of course. I'm not nearly finished. I'm not a finished angel, like you."

"What? Me? *Finished?*" I think the mountain is downside up and the lake is in the sky. And then I think, does she mean "finished," as in kaput, over and done with, out of commission? "*Finished?*"

Zola twirls one of her ribbons in her hands. "Eugenia, Bedenia." She leaps from the hammock and as she slips down through the trippy-trap door, waving the gray feather, she says, "Sa-la!"

"Sa-la," I say automatically, and then I have to float off and up into the mountains and be with the goats and find my head and the words again.

Goats

Such a world is this.

How am I not even knowing angels from peoples? I am all downside up. Maybe Zola is an angel and I am a people. I am not knowing so many things.

Maybe Zola is an angel-in-training and will replace me. Maybe I will be transferred! How awful, terrible, unfair, and ghistly! What if I get sent to places with wars and bombs?

Zola an *angel*? An *angel*? Right in my own tower all the time, an angel? Is this why she is knowing so much about angels? Is she a real angel and I am not?

I am standing in the sky with my head in the mountain.

No, *I* am the angel! I am the flisher and floater and

mostly invisible being!

But if Zola *is* an angel, then maybe she knows where the heaven is and where the angels are meeting, and maybe she knows what the rules are. I could ask her the questions.

My foot is in my ear and my head is floating away. I am not knowing anything.

The goats in the mountains are leaning against one another. *Beh, beh, beh,* they say in a comforting way. *Beh, beh, beh.* The goats are not worrying about who is an angel and who is a people or what is fair and what is ghistly. They are not worrying about what their mission is or if they will be transferred. They are just eating the grass and leaning and saying, *Beh, beh, beh.*

MORE PEOPLES

In the morning, when I return to my tower, I am still downside up, but there is much hostling and bostling going on at Casa Rosa. Off go Mr. Pomodoro and Zola in the car, while the childrens are all squibbling in the casa, waking up and bouncing soccer balls in the room of living. Paolo is in charge, which does not seem such a smart decision because he is doing most of the bouncing of the soccer balls. Two lamps are broken near the "goal" of the fireplace.

Jumpy Manuel careens from one end of the room to the other, aiming his big feet at the shizzing ball. "Pow! Pow!"

Franz shouts, "*Glocken!*" whenever he kicks the ball.

"It's not a stupid *glocken*," Paolo grumbles.

Crash.

"Oops."

Stefan lies twisty on the sofa, his head near the floor, his legs kicking at the drapes above the sofa. Josef is curled up at the other end of the sofa, trying on Mr. Pomodoro's muddy boots.

Terese is wearing two dresses, yellow over blue, and ribbons on her ankles. She is in the room of dining, casting a fishing rod.

"You will hook me," Nicola says. "Don't hook me."

Quiet Rosetta is staring mournfully out of the kitchen window.

Much of a sudden, I feel woozy, as if I have an overload of flishing in my own head. There are all these childrens here, and each one has his or her own big story inside, and each one has the childness so intrigueful, along with the absence of so much. They don't even know some things they are missing. If they had an empty drawer, they would not know what to put inside, what to save up for insurance. Should it be bread or cakes or warm gloves or soft toys or photographs? Should it be friendly words or looks or praise, but how do you put those in a drawer?

I am feeling so heavy with their stories, stories I am glompsing in splurts, detecting a bit here, a bit there. I see a tiny flash, like a speedy picture, of Franz in the basement of a bell tower, cold and shivering among the mices and roaches. I sense little Nicola falling out of a cart and lying in the mud beside the road. Manuel, I get an image of him in a closet and of big boots kicking him.

The weight of all their stories is feeling like a big crushing boulder pressing down on me, and I am wanting to push away the boulder and flish wildly so much so fast and remove all those sad things from the childrens and instead fill up their head drawers with chocolates.

And then I hear Rosetta say, "They're here. They're back. They came back." Rosetta goes into the room of living soccer field and shouts, *"They're back, you nutheads!"*

Outside, there is honk-honking, and there is Mr. Pomodoro and Zola and a lady and a boy and suitcases, and there is Signora Divino, bless her nosy nose, coming up the path, saying, "Who is? Who is?"

The childrens pour out of the house, eager to meet the newcomers, but also wary. Nicola stands to one side, ready with her warning: "Be *nice* to me!"

Signora Divino pushes her way to the front. "Who is? Who is?"

EUGENIA

Mr. Pomodoro is especially bendy as he pulls his long legs and arms from the car and arranges his face in various forms of eagerness and perplexity and fumblingness. When he introduces his wife, Eugenia, and his son, Jake, he is so proud, with cheeks rubbery smiling and eyes shining crinkly.

Signora Divino studies the little boy Jake. "Is Zola's brother! I know this in a dot!"

Aha! I think. Zola cannot be angel if so many peoples see her and she has a brother, right?

Jake, who is young like Josef, wrapples his arms around Zola's knees and buries his face in her skirt. She kneels down and squishes him in hugs. "Jakey, Jakey, Jakey," she says. "I missed you, Jickey-Jakey boy."

Aha! Zola cannot be angel! Angels do not squish peoples and tell peoples they miss them, right?

Nosy Signora Divino says to Mrs. Pomodoro, "Why so late? Why you no come before?"

Mrs. Pomodoro—Eugenia—looks like a bigger version of Zola, with chippy-choppy hair and swirly colorful skirts and scarf. She takes in the sight of the childrens draped over the steps between her and the casa.

Nicola says, "Be *nice* to me! I mean it!"

Mrs. Pomodoro turns to her husband. "I—but—is she talking to *me?*"

Signora Divino says, apparently to the air, "See? I knew there was a mama."

And then, in a surprise blipping, Mrs. Pomodoro begins speaking in zoomzoomzoom Italian to Signora Divino, who is so shockfulled that she has to sit down on the stone wall.

"No!" says Signora Divino. "No!"

"Yes," says Mrs. Pomodoro. "Swiss!"

"The niece of the daughter of Signor Pita? The Pitas who lived down the road? Those Pitas?"

"Those Pitas."

Signora Divino crosses herself. "And Bedenia Pita, bless her soul, that was your aunt?"

"Yes, Auntie Bedenia. We lived up north. We visited here."

Signora Divino taps her ears. "I remember! You were young—like Zola—yes? And now you are owning the building and making a school there?"

Mrs. Pomodoro takes a big bulp of air. "Ah, well, that . . ."

And in her hesitation I see something. I am reminded of Signora Divino, when her son's plane was *bip-bipping* in the sky, and how, afterward, she became like the egg. Maybe something like this happened to Mrs. Pomodoro, and now she is trying to be strong on the outside, but inside is fragile. She wants her family to be safe in this new place, but she is worried, too. She is a mama.

While I am thinking of the nature of mamas, I hear in the air a summons. Signor Rubini of the blue socks needs me. He is having distressment, and so I go to him.

Several hours later when I return to the casa, I see Eugenia Pomodoro unwrapping two small pickets from her suitcase. She takes them to the mantel. There she places a picture of her husband and one of Zola next to the ones of her and Jake. She presses a finger to each one, even her own.

These pictures have many fingerprints on them.

I am no sooner back on my tower balcony than clip-clop comes Zola. I am not knowing too much what is happening, but I am having some guesses.

"So," I say, "your mother's name is Eugenia."

Zola does the teeth smile and winks. "Eugenia Bedenia."

"So, she *is* your mother?"

Zola gives a horse nod, a slow down and up of her head.

"Then you are *not* an orphan?"

"Not today."

"Are you an angel today?"

Zola taps her chinny, thinking. "You are a good angel."

"I am?" I am so shockful that I nearly fall through the trippy-trap door. No one has said this to me ever. A good angel? But no, no, I don't want to get lost in the words. "Zola, you are not an angel, right?"

Zola leans against the balcony wall and stares out at the beautiful mountain, so tall and strong. She says, as if to the mountain, "Am I an angel?"

Arf, arf, arf, arf—

"Oh, no," says Zola.

Zola's brother is running toward the *arf*ing dog.

Arf, arf, arf, arf—

"Jakey, be careful!" Swiftly, Zola clambers down through the trippy-trap door.

I am there in a swiftness.

Arf, arf, oof, eef, rrmm—

The *arf*ing *il beasto* has rolled over onto his back and is letting Jake rub his pancia—pancho—what you call it?—stomaco? *Rrmm—rmm—*

Signora Divino appears at the gate and sees Jake patting *il beasto*'s pancho-stomaco. She says, "Jake-o, you—you are *un angelo*! An angel!"

Zola turns to me and gives me the many-teeth-smalling smile.

My head, it has flown off to the moon. Is *everyone* an angel?

PIGEONS

That night I am flinging here and there on the balcony, all mixed up about peoples and angels. In the morning, though, while Mr. Pomodoro is showing his wife the progressing of the school building, I see all the childrens in the house, and I am knowing that the talking and touching and seeing each other is what peoples do, not angels.

I am having a sad feeling.

Paolo and Zola are helping the other childrens make pretty eggs—like Easter eggs, except it is not Easter. It is August. Where do childrens find these ideas? Soon they have wax and crayons and string and so many things on the table that it is a bigga mess.

And then when Zola and Paolo are in the kitchen

getting more eggs, Zola's little brother Jake smashes his egg on the table in the room of dining and Josef does the same, and then they smoosh the crumbling pieces of egg and shell into the tiny cracks of the table because it looks pretty, those yellow and white tracks, and then Nicola smashes her egg, and Rosetta does the same.

Jake is intrigueful of his crumbly egg and tries some on his face and Josef does the same and then puts some in his hairs. Nicola tries some in her ear while Rosetta puts some nicely on her feets. Zola and Paolo return from the kitchen and stand there with their mouths stuck in open position.

"Jake!" Zola says. "Nicola! Rosetta! Josef!"

The childrens beam, so surpleased with their smooshed eggs, and Zola says, "If you weren't so squishy cute and rosy cheeky, I would kick each of you in your rumpy!"

In the early evening when Zola arrives through the trippy-trap door on the balcony of the tower, she says, "Angel, I will tell you something."

At first I think she is going to tell me something else I have to do, but instead she tells me about when her brother, Jake, was born.

"It was such a night as this," Zola says, "this kind of sky, this kind of warm air, but no mountains. Jake came way too early—two months!"

"I have seen babies like that, Zola. In such a hurry . . ."

"We were afraid."

"Yes, Zola, peoples get afraid when—"

Zola makes a rubber mouth like her father. "Angel, please. Let me just tell this, okay?"

Well! I was only trying to be a good hearing aid and contribute something now and then to show the sympathy.

"Angel, we were afraid for Jake, such a tiny, tiny baby. When finally I got to see him, he was in an incubator: a tiny, shriveled bird no bigger than this"—Zola cups her hands together—"with wires poking here and there, such a skinny puny pitiful thing."

Zola pauses, but I am not sure if I can talk yet, so I say nothing.

"Angel, on the top of the incubator, just above Jake's shriveled head, someone had fastened a miniature golden angel, maybe from a necklace or something. The angel was gazing down into the incubator."

Zola glances at me in the expecting way, and so I think it is my turn. "Oh," I say, "that is a nice thing, that angel on the incubator."

"But, wait," Zola says. "While I am standing there, an eerie glow of blue-white light appears in the corner of the room, and the glow comes closer and closer to the incubator, and then it moves up to the ceiling and hovers there."

"You didn't see any frogs?"

"What? *Frogs?* No, I did not see any frogs, Angel! Just listen—"

"Hokay, hokay."

Zola is leaning on the balcony wall. "While I am watching shriveled Jake, the blue-white light comes and soon it takes shape. I rub my eyes. It appears—now don't get mad, Angel. . . ."

"Why would I get mad? I won't get mad."

"Angel, the blue-white light became—well, it looked like—a pigeon."

"A pigeon?"

"Yes."

"A *pigeon?*"

"Yes. It was still fuzzy around the edges and still all blue-white, but it gave off a very comforting feeling, and I knew it was an angel."

"An angel?"

"Yes."

"Zola, a pigeon is not an angel."

"Well, yes, it might seem that way, but this angel—".

"Zola, angels are not pigeons!"

"I knew you would get mad."

"I am not mad."

"You are."

"Not." But I *am* mad. How can peoples go around thinking angels are pigeons, or pigeons are angels?

"Do you want to hear more?" Zola asks.

What I really want is to float up into the mountains to see the goats and stop from hearing the nonsense about the pigeons, but I am a polite angel most of the time and so I say, "Of course. Go on talking."

"So we did not know if shriveled Jake would live, not for this minute or this hour or this night or that day. Every minute, every day we are watching his tiny chest go up and down, and in our heads we are saying, 'Don't stop, keep going,' and always there is the blue-white pigeon—"

"Do you have to call it a pigeon?"

"But that's what it looked like to me. Remember, I was only six years old—"

"Couldn't you call it maybe just 'the light'?"

"Angel! Try not to be so bothered by the pigeon. To me it looked like a pigeon, a fuzzy one, with a beautiful halo of light all around it. And every day and every night, the pigeon—the *pigeon*—was there, and I felt it was protecting Jake and that it was an angel—"

"But a pigeon is not—"

"Just listen, please! I felt that this thing—this light—this *pigeon*—was an angel and it was protecting Jake, and I was so glad it was there, especially when I could not be there. And then one day, the wires and monitors were removed and Jake was breathing all on his own and opening his eyes and taking a bottle and waving his fingers, and that's when the blue light left."

"The pigeon."

"Yes."

"The pigeon went away."

"Yes."

I cannot help myself. I have to ask Zola one more question. "Zola? Do you think *I* look like a pigeon?"

LIZARDS

~~~

Spring and summer is lizard time here in the mountains. The lizards are small and narrow, like green worms with feets and tails. No, cuter than that. Tiny heads that turn this way and that, watching, listening. Tiny feets, so dainty. Slender tails, so wispy. The lizards sun themselves on the rock walls, dartling into slim crevices when peoples or animals near. *Zip. Zip.* Freeze. *Zip.*

In the middle of the night, Paolo summons Zola.

"Rosetta ate a lizard."

"She did what?"

"She ate a lizard."

Rosetta is curled in a ball on her bed, sobbing. "I die, I die."

"Now, now," says Zola. "You won't die. What happened?"

Manuel kicks the side of Rosetta's bed. "She ate a lizard. They going to cut her open to get it out."

Rosetta shrieks.

Zola says, "Rosetta, did you truly eat a lizard?"

Manuel answers for her. "She did, and they going to cut her open to get it out."

Rosetta shrieks and sobs.

Zola scoots onto the bed and cuddles Rosetta. "Rosetta, tell me. Why did you eat a lizard?"

"Not whole lizard," Rosetta says between sobs. "Just tail."

Manuel feels it necessary to explain to Franz and Terese, who have been awakened by the noise, that Rosetta has eaten a lizard and will have to have her stomach cut open.

"Really?" they say.

Rosetta sobs.

"Rosetta, please tell me. Why did you eat the lizard?"

"Not whole lizard. Just tail. Because it was so cute and little."

"They cut your stomach open," Manuel insists.

Zola says, "Nonsense. A little lizard tail won't hurt anyone."

Terese leans over and throws up on the orange rug.

Zola says, "Did you eat some lizard, too?"

Terese is gagging. She cannot answer.

"Anyone else in here eat lizard?" Zola asks.

Franz puts his hand to his stomach. "I ate some wax."

Josef has crawled out of bed to see what is happening. "I ate a spider once."

I retreat to my balcony. It's just a normal night with childrens.

THE MAYOR

Today everyone—Zola and her family and the childrens and the villagers—gather at the old Pita building, which soon will be the School of Pomodoro. In each room, peoples are painting or cleaning or hammering, and there is much clanging and banging and whooping.

Vinny has brought his drums. "Entertainment!" he says, but I think maybe he doesn't want to work. He only wants to play the drums. Rosetta, the lizard eater, hangs by his side, tapping her fingers on the windowsill.

Signora Divino, with a jauntly pink scarf around her neckle and a blue ribbon on her wrist, is slinging pits and pots in the new kitchen of the school, and while she is slanging and clattering, she is telling Zola's mother in zoomzoom Italian that the Pomodoros should talk with her son, Massimo, and his wife, Bette, and all of them should open the school together, and that way Vinny and Massimo and Bette could stay right here.

"This is where they need to be," Signora Divino says. "Here! You agree? Of course you agree."

I am feeling most hopeful watching these peoples. I don't know what to say about this feeling. I don't eat food, but if I did, maybe it is as if I was hungry, so hungry, and I didn't even know it, and then I found a mountain of food and I ate and ate, and then I sat back contentful and there was still more mountain for the next day and the next day. Maybe it is like that. I don't know. Since I don't eat food, it is hard to say.

Into this merry confusion of peoples painting and cleaning, struddles Mayor Zapino, home from his vacation. He is a round man: round head, round eyes, round nose, round belly. He carries thick envelopes with him, which he wivvles in the air as he demands to see Mr. Pomodoro.

"The children must go!" he says. "The school no opens!"

"Pardon?" says Mr. Pomodoro.

"No permissions! No *passaportos*! No *scuola*!" Mayor

Zapino's cheeks poof out importantly.

Mr. Pomodoro squinches his face. "We have permissions, Mr. Mayor."

The mayor flickers his fingers at his collar. "Zapino! Mayor Zapino!"

Signora Divino rushes into the room, waving a pot. "Idiot!"

The childrens are afraid. They creep out the door, one dribble, two dribble, slinking along the side of the building. I flish in their heads: to the rock, to the tower, my tower.

Soon they are all gathered in the lower tower room. They are huddled and quiet. Nicola stands stubbornly in the middle of the room, her arms crossed.

Zola clabbers up through the trippy-trap door. "Angel!" she says.

"I know, I know," I say. "'Do something!' That's what you're going to say, right? Why do *I* always have to do the somethings? Why don't *you* do something?"

And just then, right that moment, there is a gray flutter and on the ledge of the tower balcony lands a pigeon.

Yes. A pigeon.

Zola looks at me. I look at Zola. We both look at the pigeon.

It is sleek and smooth, with iridescent (is that the word for the sparkly shine?) feathers: gray on top but luminous red and green underneath, and when the pigeon moves its head, you see those colors flashing, and the light spickles off the smooth feathers so that the bird appears to glow. There seems to be, I almost hate to say this, but there seems to be a blue-white light around the pigeon.

"Do something!" I say to the pigeon. The pigeon cocks his head so that I can see the powerful red and green shimmery feathers. Then I am a bit worried. What if this pigeon is my superior? What if it is a chief angel?

And even though I do not believe that pigeons are angels, in that minute, beholding that pigeon, I am not so sure, and so I say to Zola, "I will see what I can do. You and—and—the pigeon stay here and watch the childrens, hokay?" And off I zip, in my most commanding way, swoosh, a blaze of light. I am hoping the pigeon will be impressified.

LUIGI

Signora Divino slaps Mayor Zapino on the arm. "What would your nice mama think of you now? You stop this."

I am ready to flish in the heads, but before I can do this, Eugenia Pomodoro enters, carrying a rolling pin in one hand and a paintbrush in the other. She peers at the mayor.

"Luigi? Is it you?"

Mayor Zapino, who is rubbing his arm from Signora Divino's slap, turns red in the face cheeks. "Who is this?"

"Luigi! It *is* you!"

The eyes of the mayor look as if they will roll out of his head. "Eugenia?"

"Luigi!"

"Eugenia!"

Mr. Pomodoro raises his hand as if he needs permission to speak. "Eugenia?"

Mrs. Pomodoro does not see the raised hand of her husband. She is so happy to see the mayor. "Luigi, Luigi!"

"Eugenia, Eugenia!"

Mayor Zapino and Mrs. Pomodoro hug and kiss each other three times on the cheeks: right, left, right.

Mr. Pomodoro repeats, "Eugenia?"

And then Eugenia Pomodoro, with her chippy-choppy hair, introduces her old school chum, Luigi Zapino, to her husband. "Luigi was in Geneva three years when my family was there. Luigi, Luigi! My dear Luigi!"

Mayor Zapino is now many colors of red in his face and neck. "This Pomodoro is your husband?"

"Yes," Eugenia says.

"You own this building?"

"Yes. Auntie Bedenia left it to me."

"Ah, Auntie Bedenia," the mayor says, with a soft beam in his eye. "She gave us the licorices when we visited her, remember?" The mayor suddenly seems to recall his duty. He makes himself taller by stretching his neck. "I am sorry, but the orphan children, they are not legal, they must return . . ."

Zola enters from the side door, swinging her arms. She is determined about something. Paolo follows her.

"Mr. Mayor," Zola says.

Paolo echoes Zola. "Mr. Mayor."

The mayor continues speaking to the Pomodoros.

"As I was saying, since the orphan children are not legal . . ."

Zola steps forward. "Mr. Mayor. Mr. Mayor. Mr. Mayor."

Paolo also steps forward. "Mr. Mayor."

"What? What *is* it? What do you want?" The mayor's round red cheeks are puffing in and out.

"I am Zola."

"I am Paolo."

The mayor is most flustered. "What? You are interrupting. I am busy here."

Zola's eyes flash from ceiling to floor, from Mama to Papa, from villager to villager.

"Mr. Mayor," Zola says. "It is most important that we ask you this question."

"What? Get on with it! I have business—"

"Mr. Mayor, would you like some ravioli?"

"Ravioli?"

Zola turns to Signora Divino. "Signora Divino, this morning you made the best ravioli. Don't you think the mayor would like some?" Zola wizzles her eyebrows at Signora Divino in a most significanting way.

Signora Divino waves her pot in the air. "He stay for ravioli, or I knock him on the head."

Such a Day

S uch a day, such a day!

The Pomodoros and Signora Divino and the villagers stuff Mayor Zapino so full of ravioli, and Mrs. Pomodoro stuffs him so full of good memories of being childrens together that the mayor feels surely all the permissions for the school and the childrens will be in fine order, absolutemento! I only do a small amount of flishing in the mayor's head; mostly it is the peoples who do the flishing. I am impressified.

The childrens are so perlieved to hear that they will not be sent away to live in a ditch that they all start drumming—with sticks and hairbrushes and spoons and whatever they can find—in a loud song of celebration. "Yay, we stay! *Glocken, glocken, glocken!* Yay, we stay!" It is most noiseful, the air full of *booms* and *clangs* and *pomps* and *clacks.*

And *I* am perlieved to report that Zola does not think I look like a pigeon. The pigeon that came to the tower is gone, leaving behind only a stray feather and some white slopping. If it was an angel, it must have decided that we were doing finely on our own, and if it was not an angel, it was just a pigeon that was free to go whenever it liked. I think it was just a pigeon.

WHAT THE ANGEL KNOWS

Skirtling along one side of the paths and lanes cut into our mountainside are stone walls. These stone walls keep clumpy mud and rocks from falling on the paths and the peoples. Spaced here and there in the walls, in a pleasingful pattern, are holes. Am I saying this right? Holes in the walls. Each the size of a brick maybe. Here and there. Can you see it?

I like these holes very much. When too much rain pours down, the water has a place to sneak out. When peoples approach a lizard sunning himself on the wall, the lizard has a place to run and hide. When the peoples want surpleases of blossoms in those hard stone walls, they plant violets and other dainty purple and blue and white flowers. But childrens love these holes most of all, for there they can hide the secret notes and the tiny treasures. And the big peoples like this because they can be walking along and peek inside a wall hole and see a folded note or maybe a bracelet of colorful plastic beads or a stash of pinecones or smooth pebbles.

Who thought of these holes when building these walls? I am liking those peoples.

For the last years, ten or twenty, the holes have been dried up and empty except for dirt clogs and lizards. Today, though, I notice a folded note inside one hole and a piece of red cloth inside another. I see near Signora Pompa's house the bluebells sprouting out, draping down the gray stone wall. I see Josef and Jakey with Vinny Divino, peering inside a hole, poking with a stick. I see Franz the *glocken* boy pick up a dead mouse and gently tuck it inside a wall hole and then carefully place thick, green leaves over the opening. He then removes one leaf and with a twig carves a cross on it and returns it to the wall hole.

The childrens, they are spickling up the sleepy village, teasing it awake again. It is like the dust of magic drifting down over the mountain.

And while I am feeling contentful watching the wall holes being filled with treasures, I get a sudden sorrow feeling, missing all the childrens and their mamas and papas and grandmas and grandpas who have come and gone, come and gone. It is hard work watching over the peoples and flishing and wishing them safely.

Sometimes I feel that I have to be like the mountain, rock strong, and on the inside I have to have the arsenal ready to fight invaders who might hurt my peoples. And I don't even have a sword.

And then, how this happens is always a surprisement, but I see something that makes me feel like a softly melting mountain. It might be Nicola, crossing the lawn of Casa Rosa, pumping her little arms, dressed in a yellow skirt and a blue one and a turquoise blouse too big and a red scarf around her waist. She is pumping along, heading for the path, and she is singing a song: "I hate zucchini, zucchini, zucchini. I hate green glop, green glop, green glop," and in her hand she is carrying green glop in a wet napkin. She places this glop in the nearest wall hole, wipes her hands on her skirt, spots a lizard running along the wall and follows it until it slips into another wall hole.

Childrens.

There is Paolo, strutting along the alleyway and up the stone drive, running his hand along the wall, casually peering into each of the holes. He stops, glances around, and removes a folded white paper from his sleeve. Again he glances this way, that way, and then his hand darts into the hole, depositing the paper.

How can I *not* look? On the paper one name is

written over and over and over: *Zola Zola Zola Zola Zola Zola*. Ah, Paolo.

Further up the path, Zola is dancing along, looking for just the right wall hole. Not this one. Not that one. Ah, there is one, up there. From her pocket, she pulls a white something and quickly stuffs it into the hole. She snatches a clomp of moss and plugs the hole with it.

Hokay, so I am nosy. After Zola leaves, I take a look. It is a small white statue of an angel with broken arms. I have seen this on the long table in the alley, when the villagers gathered items for the childrens. Poor little broken-armed angel.

I am in my tower that overlooks the village: all the stone buildings and walls and casas and peoples and animals. I am mostly sure this is my territory, and I hope I will not get transferred. I will be flishing in the minds if I need to so the childrens can stay here and go to school and be warm and not hungry. I will visit the old peoples in the night and calm them, and I will watch over Signora Divino and Vinny and throw pinecones when needed, but I hope *il beasto* gets hit by a truck. No! I do not mean it. But I do wish he would lose his *arf*.

I am gladful Zola came to my tower. I like to be in her energy. Sometimes a people needs an angel and sometimes an angel needs a people. I am also gladful the childrens came to our village. Sometimes old peoples need young peoples and young peoples need old peoples.

Of course there will still be the *pocketa-pocketa* and the *boom-boom-boom* and the talking all the time and the painted feets of the peoples.

Peoples: so unfinished!

Ah. Peoples! Angels!

The Unfinished Angel

Learn How to Talk Like the Unfinished Angel

"Dictionary" Definitions

A Q&A Session with Sharon Creech

Incredilish Hardness Word Search!

Learn How to Talk Like the Unfinished Angel

The angel's language:
In Switzerland, while I was immersed in relearning Italian (the language of southern Switzerland), I found myself talking strangely and comically, mixing English and Italian and mangling grammar in both languages. Not only could I not speak Italian correctly, but I could no longer speak English correctly! The two languages were so tangled in my brain. An example: I'd need the word *attractive*, but I couldn't find that exact word. Instead, I'd think of attractiful or attracting. The only way this story was going to get written was if I let the angel speak the way my brain was working that year!

—Sharon Creech

Do you tire of the dry language you use in your everyday life? Add flair to your words by learning to talk like the Unfinished Angel!

1. Invent gibberish-sounding words that resemble actual words in English.

- Body = bedy, bidy, budy
- Mouse = meuse, miuse, mause
- Run = ren, ron, rin

1

2. Make numerous statements with your "angel" language.

I went for my daily jeg around the park today. No, what is that word for the fasting walk? Jig? Jag?? Jug? No, jog! Jog!

"Dictionary" Definitions

Weave the angel's language into your daily conversations! This short guide defines and provides examples for the angel's favorite nonsense words.

Peoples *noun*: a large group of people.
> <Those *peoples* are causing a ruckus!>

Childrens *noun*: children, little kids.
> <*Childrens!* Please stop hogging the playground!>

Adulterinos *noun*: adults. A fun way to refer to your parents, teachers, elders, and grandparents; the possibilities are endless!
> <But . . . *adulterino* . . . you remember what it was like to be my age, right?>

Extraremarkable *adjective*: an extraordinary event. Used to describe any person, place, or thing that is beyond the typical.
> <I had an *extraremarkable* day today! I snagged the last chocolate pudding cup at lunch and rounded the bases in kickball!>

Mashmish *noun*: a muddled mess. Refers to anyone or anything that is unappealing, messy, or a failed mix of many things.

> <This meatloaf is a giant *mashmish* of ketchup, meat, and my mother's lack of cooking skills. Ack!>

Suprisement *noun*: an unexpected event. Can be good or bad, depending on the situation.

> <I was less than delighted to find a *suprisement* waiting for me on the kitchen counter when I got home—an empty jar of cookies.>

Incredilish *adjective*: incredible, amazing. An event, person, place, or thing that is above and beyond "exciting" or "wonderful."

> <Molly is so *incredilish*! She expertly plays the piano with her elbows and makes amazing peanut butter cookies!>

A Q&A Session with Sharon Creech

What sparked your imagination for THE UNFINISHED ANGEL?
I'd been trying to write a book about an angel ever since 2003, when my then two-year-old granddaughter told her first story: "Once upon a time in Spain there was an angel, and the angel was me. The end." I loved that and wanted to know more about that angel, but I couldn't "catch" the voice or the story until nearly five years later when I went to Switzerland for the year with my husband. We were staying on the campus of the TASIS school in Montagnola (also the setting for BLOOMABILITY), and one of the most prominent features of the campus is a tall, old stone tower attached to a villa. As soon as I saw that tower, I knew it was where the angel would live.

View from the angel's tower

The angel's tower

The "chicken shad" where the orphans are first found

You have written both novels and picture books. How does the writing process differ for each genre?

A picture book feels more like a poem, in which one clear image is rendered in the fewest, purest words. It is not easy to write a *memorable* picture book. The images that come to me are more often suited to the larger canvas of the novel, where there is more room for parallels and contrasts and complications. I like to roam.

What challenges do you face in your writing process? How do you overcome them?

The challenges change and evolve. Right now, the biggest challenge is being able to clear the decks and make time for the extended work a novel requires. I like to be immersed in the story and to be free of obligations—no company, no events, no travel, no cooking, no cleaning! My head needs to fill up with the book, and when it does, there is little room for anything else. Fortunately, my friends and family know there are times when I need to be in the world of the book, and they let me go there.

How did your experiences as a high school teacher impact your writing career?

I learned more about story and about people during those teaching years than I did in all my previous years of formal education. I saw what interested readers and what did not, and I learned how alike we all are—whether from Japan or Germany or Spain or America or China or Russia—and also how unique each individual truly is.

How do you decide on themes for your books?
When I was in school I hated that word "theme"—I didn't understand it. My impression of the theme of a given book was never what the teacher said it was, nor would it fit into a compact phrase. If the writer did not say, "This is my theme," then how could there be one "right" theme?

I never think about theme. To me, books are about people and places, and a story is the following of a group of people in a particular time and place. I'm not able to say what my own themes are, but if readers want to suggest some, they are certainly welcome to do so. Just know that there are no "wrong" ones.

How important is research in the development of your books? Can you explain the process as well?
Ah, research. This is another area that is hard to define and explain. Often, it feels as if most of my research has already been done before I'm aware that I will write a particular story. This is because the characters and places that interest me for stories arise from people I have encountered and places I have lived or visited. When I begin to reshape these "known" elements into story, I want pure imagination to be at work. I don't want to be limited by "research," by facts.

Having said all that, though, every book requires some checking of facts, and this I do in lulls between chapters. Sometimes I will set off for a place (Switzerland, Kentucky, England) to refresh my memory or I will consult reference books, but I try not to let the research overtake the initial impulses for the story.

What tips or advice can you share with young students who hope to start writing?
Read a lot and write a lot. It's simple advice, but it works. You don't have to know "the story" before you begin. Feel free to experiment, to try a lot of different styles and topics, and to have fun. Write about the people and places and things that interest you. You can start with anything—with that stone or that gate or that dog or that man. Don't feel that anything has to be perfect or that everything has to be finished.

Can you suggest a fun writing topic to get them started?
Choose a painting or photograph that interests you and pretend that you are either a person in the photograph or someone on the edge of the scene. Describe what you see and what you are thinking.

I like this exercise because the artist or photographer has already selected composition, color, tone, detail, mood, and if you now render the same image(s) in words, you are likely to come up with something intriguing.

Incredilish Hardness Word Search!

```
t s p p a i n m s z p c e s o
s m r p o m o d o r o o d l p
r s i a n c o u u b h d z i a
r w e i i z k m o s g o l s u
a i l i v a o e o s n b o w m
o t p y i o p l t i e o a s f
a z z n d n c p a a r k w r s
l e g n a d e h s i n i f n u
s r n i r s o t o o s o a n e
c l s v o k o r r s i n b a e
n a i g n i f r a r t b g p e
n n w s g r i l s e l p o e p
e d i n i t p o a e s m l o s
o n o l s s p n c w i s i b m
s i i z o y p a l t v m l l g
```

arfing

mr. pomodoro

skirts

boom

peoples

swiss alps

casa rosa

pocketa

switzerland

il beasto

signora divino

unfinished angel

vinny

zola

Read all of the classics by Newbery Medal winner
Sharon Creech!

- *Walk Two Moons*—Newbery Medal Winner
- *The Wanderer*—Newbery Honor Book
- *Ruby Holler*—Carnegie Medal Winner
- *The Boy on the Porch*
- *The Great Unexpected*
- *Absolutely Normal Chaos*
- *Pleasing the Ghost*
- *Chasing Redbird*
- *Bloomability*
- *Love That Dog*
- *Granny Torrelli Makes Soup*
- *Heartbeat*
- *Replay*
- *The Castle Corona*
- *Hate That Cat*
- *The Unfinished Angel*

www.sharoncreech.com

Joanna Cotler Books
An Imprint of HarperCollinsPublishers

HARPER
An Imprint of HarperCollinsPublishers